OPENING NIGHT
ON THE MYSTERY PLANET...

The earthmen had presented their opera for the "people" of Zade. Now it was the turn of the Zadans to put on a performance:

Jets of flame thrust up from the floor; iron rails fell from above to crash into the aisles. Six razor-edged pendulums were released from above, and swung back and forth over the heads of the audience. A great boulder toppled from above, to be caught by a chain inches from the heads of the panic-stricken visitors from Earth. Down from the trusses dropped chunks of red-hot iron. . . .

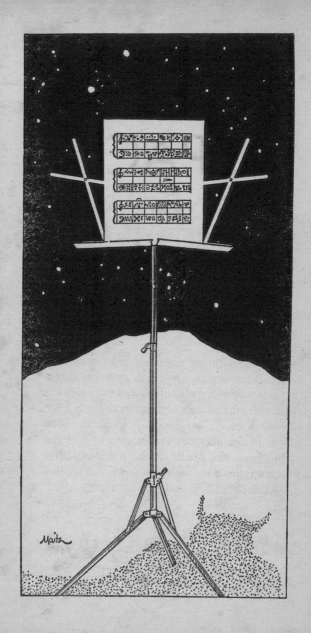

SPACE
OPERA

Jack Vance

DAW BOOKS, INC.
DONALD A. WOLLHEIM, PUBLISHER

1301 Avenue of the Americas
New York, N.Y.   10019

FIRST DAW PRINTING, APRIL 1979

1 2 3 4 5 6 7 8 9

PRINTED IN U.S.A.

SPACE OPERA

Chapter One

ROGER WOOL, sitting to the rear of his aunt's box at the Palladian Theater, poured himself a third glass of champagne. Dame Isabel Grayce, occupied with her two guests, failed to notice and Roger sat back with a pleasant sense of accomplishment.

Five minutes to curtain time! The air was rich with golden light, heavy with a delicious expectancy. After triumphs elsewhere around the world, the Ninth Company of Rlaru at last had come to the Palladian. Everyone knew of their distinctive programs, which were like nothing ever before seen on Earth; some charming and wistful, others projecting an almost terrible sense of doom.

Augmenting popular interest in the Ninth Company was the controversy which had accompanied them around the world: was the troupe genuinely the product of a far planet, or did they represent a hoax perpetrated by an exceedingly clever set of musicians? Everywhere critics and experts were divided. The evidence of the music was ambiguous: in some respects it seemed absolutely alien; in others it appeared hauntingly similar to certain Earth musics.

Roger Wool had hardly bothered to form an opinion; but Dame Isabel Grayce, Secretary-Treasurer of the Opera League, was more deeply involved; indeed, only her sponsorship had secured Adolph Gondar entrée into the theaters and opera houses of the world. At the moment Dame Isabel was engaged in a stiff conversation with her two guests. These were Joseph Lewis Thorpe, music critic for the *Transatlantic Times,* and Elgin Seaboro, theatrical edi-

1

tor of the *Galactic Review*. Both had written cynically in
regard to the Ninth Company without troubling to attend a
performance, and Dame Isabel had insisted that they repair the deficiency.

The curtain parted to reveal an empty stage. The impresario, Adolph Gondar, stepped forward: a tall dark man
with a saturnine forehead, brooding black eyes, a long
melancholy jaw and chin: not a man to inspire confidence,
but by the same token, not a man to whom such large-
scale chicanery would come easily. He spoke perfunctory
words and left the stage. After several electric moments the
orchestral members of the Ninth Troupe appeared, went
to a dais at one side of the stage, almost idly picked up instruments and began to play. The music was thin and
sweet, and tonight it seemed almost gay.

Presently others of the troupe came forth to present a
merry little operetta, so casual as to seem impromptu, yet
precisely timed and exquisite in regard to polish and flair.
The plot? It could never be stated in words; perhaps there
was none. Roger enjoyed the presentation and wondered
what all the fuss was about. The performers seemed not
quite human, though close enough for empathy. They were
flexible and frail, and somehow one received the impression that their internal organs were different in formation and arrangement from those of Earth-folk. The men
were straight, sinewy, with startling white skins, blazing
black eyes and sleek black hair. The women were softer,
delightfully shaped, with piquant little faces half-hidden in
puffs of black hair. They pranced gaily from one side of
the stage to the other, singing in sweet plaintive voices,
changing costumes with bewildering celerity, while the
men stood stern and stiff, facing in various directions or
whirling about in accordance with a definite but incompre-
hensible set of canons. Meanwhile other members of the
troupe provided music, a fragile polyphony sometimes
seeming mere random sound, then just as the suspicion approached certainty, resolving into a set of ravishing chords
which explained and ordered all which had gone before.

Pleasant, if puzzling, thought Roger Wool, pouring himself another glass of champagne. The bottle clinked in the ice and Dame Isabel swung around her formidable glance. Roger replaced the bottle with exaggerated caution.

Presently the performance halted for intermission. Dame Isabel turned from Joseph Lewis Thorpe to Elgin Seaboro with an austere and challenging air of triumph. "Your doubts and misgivings are erased, or so I trust?"

Joseph Lewis Thorpe cleared his throat, glanced at Elgin Seaboro. "Virtuosity of a sort. Indeed, indeed, indeed."

Elgin Seaboro said, "No question but what we have here a clever and daring group, rather well integrated. Fresh new talent, I would say. Competely fresh."

"This is a fair pronouncement," stated Thorpe.

Dame Isabel knit her brows. "You agree then that Adolph Gondar and the Ninth Troupe are genuine?"

Joseph Lewis Thorpe laughed uneasily. "My dear lady, I can only reiterate that I find his conduct the opposite of reassuring. Why will he allow no press interviews? Why has not some ethnologist of reputation examined these people? The circumstances do not conduce to easy acceptance of Mr. Gondar's claims."

"You think then that Mr. Gondar has hoodwinked me? After all, the whole tour has been under my supervision; I control all financial matters, and I doubt if you can seriously accuse me of peccancy."

"My dear lady, there is not the slightest hint of such a thing!" declared Thorpe. "You are almost notoriously straight-forward!"

"Adolph Gondar may well be an excellent fellow," chimed in Seaboro, "aside from his attempt to pull the wool over our eyes."

"Yes," said Thorpe. "Exactly who is Gondar?"

Dame Isabel compressed her lips and Roger watched fascinated. "Mr. Gondar," she said with great distinctness, "is a sensitive and perspicacious man. His trade is that of a spaceship captain. He has visited dozens of far worlds. On one of these, that world called Rlaru, he managed to prevail upon the Ninth Company to undertake a tour of

Earth. That is all there is to it. I cannot understand your skepticism, especially after my reassurances."

Seaboro gave a hearty laugh. "It is our business to be skeptical. Who ever heard of a credulous critic?"

"My objections," said Thorpe, "are based partly on musical theory, and partly on an informed layman's knowledge of the galaxy. I find it hard to believe that an alien race can employ a comprehensible musical idiom, and also I have never heard mention of the planet 'Rlaru' which presumably exhibits a highly advanced civilization."

"Ah," said Dame Isabel, eyelids hooding her eyes—a signal which caused Roger to wince uneasily. "Then you believe these performers to be ordinary earth-people masquerading as aliens?"

Seaboro shrugged. "As to that I can't say. All of us have seen presentations which appear miraculous, but which we know to be clever stage management. These people show no strikingly non-human characteristics. If you identified them as the graduating class of the Golliwog Cakewalk Academy of Earthville on Procyon Planet, I would not disbelieve you."

"You are a fool," said Dame Isabel, with the air of one pronouncing a considered and final judgment.

Seaboro sniffed, swung around in his seat. Thorpe laughed nervously. "Unfair! Unfair! We are all mere mortals pushing through our various dark thickets! Bernard Bickel, who probably knows—"

Dame Isabel made a sound of intense annoyance. "Don't mention that name to me!" she snapped. "He is an opinionated *poseur,* completely superficial."

"He is probably the world's leading authority on comparative musicology," stated Seaboro coldly. "We cannot help but be influenced by his views."

Dame Isabel sighed. "I might have expected no more." And now once more the curtain was rising on the stage.

The Ninth Company presented a *fête champêtre.* In garments of pink and blue, green and blue, yellow and blue diaper, the players were engaging hybrids of fairies and harlequins. As before there seemed no plot, no perceptible pattern of movement. The music was a chirping, twiddling, tinkling confection occasionally underscored by a hoarse booming like a foghorn's tone, or the blast of a conch. From side to side moved the players, this way and that: a pavanne? A bucolic celebration? The apparently aimless motion, the curtsies, the frivolous capering and cantering continued without development or alteration, but suddenly came the startling intuition that here was no farce, no gentle entertainment, but a presentment of something somber and terrible: an evocation of heart-rending sadness. The lights faded to darkness. A flash of dazzling blue-green light revealed the Ninth Company in attitudes of attention and inquiry, as if they themselves were perplexed by the problem they had propounded. When the audience could see once more the curtain had fallen and the music had stopped.

"Clever," muttered Thorpe. "Though inchoate."

"I note a certain absence of discipline," Seaboro reported. "A praiseworthy exuberance, an attempt to break away from traditional forms, but, as you say, inchoate."

"Good evening, Madame Grayce," said Thorpe. "Thank you very much for your invitation. Good evening to you, sir." The latter was addressed to Roger.

Elgin Seaboro echoed his colleague's remarks; the two departed.

Dame Isabel rose to her feet. "A pair of buffoons. Come, Roger."

"I believe I will leave you here," said Roger. "I have an engagement—"

"You have nothing of the sort. You are driving me to Lillian Monteagle's supper party."

Roger Wood acquiesced. He was dependent, to a great degree, upon his aunt's largesse and found it expedient to oblige her in various small ways. They left the box, ascended to the roof, and Roger's modest little Herlingfoss Skycar was brought up from the parking pit. Dame Isabel, declining the proffer of Roger's hand, climbed grandly into the front seat.

Lillian Monteagle lived across the river in an ancient

palace which she had restored to contemporary standards of comfort. Almost as wealthy as Dame Isabel, she was famous for her elaborate entertainments, although the supper party of this particular evening was a comparatively informal occasion. Whether through innocence or light-hearted malice, Lillian Monteagle had likewise invited Bernard Bickel, the eminent musicologist, space-traveler, lecturer and *bon-vivant* to her supper.

Dame Isabel acknowledged the introduction with a barely perceptible compression of the lips, and made no mention of her connection with Adolph Gondar and the Ninth Company of Rlaru.

Inevitably the subject arose; indeed Lillian Monteagle herself, with a mischievous side-glance toward Dame Isabel, inquired if Mr. Bickel had attended the presentations which were evoking such a stir.

Bernard Bickel smilingly shook his head. He was a handsome man of early middle-age, with steel gray hair, a crisp mustache, a confident air of easy charm. "I saw a moment or two of the act on television, but I gave it no great attention. I fear that the good people of Earth are only too anxious for diversion for novelty, for anything fashionable and faddish. More power to this Adolph Gondar: if idle and foolish folk are willing to pay him, why should he not take the money?"

"My dear Mr. Bickel," protested Lillian Monteagle, "you sound as if you doubted the authenticity of this troupe!"

Bernard Bickel smiled quietly. "I'll say this much: I have never heard of the planet 'Rlaru,' or however it's pronounced. And, as you know, I have traveled space a great deal."

A young lady across the table leaned forward. "But Mr. Bickel! I think you're being dreadfully unfair! You haven't even gone to one of the performances! I have, and I was absolutely thrilled."

Bernard Bickel shrugged. "Adolph Gondar, whoever or whatever he may be, undoubtedly is a fantastically good showman."

Dame Isabel cleared her throat. Roger relaxed in his chair: why give way to tension or nervousness? What would be, would be; Dame Isabel, by virtue of age, sex, and commanding presence, usually emerged with dignity intact and the opposition cowed. She spoke. "I must take issue with you. Adolph Gondar is totally inept as a showman, though he is probably a competent captain of spaceships, for this is his trade."

"Oh?" Bernard Bickel cocked one of his eyebrows into a quizzical arch. "This would of course lend color to his claims. As for myself—" he lifted his wine, inspected the scarlet shine "—modesty aside, I am close to the top of a field which has been variously called comparative musicology, symbological euphonics, or just plain musicology. And I simply refuse to be hornswoggled by the mysterious Adolph Gondar. His music is comprehensible, which is the give-away. Music is like a language: you cannot understand it unless you learn it, or more accurately, are born into it."

"Hear, hear!" said someone softly. Dame Isabel swung her head about in an effort to identify the offender. She said in a frosty voice, "Do you refuse to believe, then, that sensitive and intelligent creatures of one world are unable to comprehend the artistic efforts—including the music— of equally sensitive and intelligent inhabitants of another world?"

Bernard Bickel realized that he had caught a Tartar, and decided upon retreat. "No, of course not. Not at all. I recall an amusing adventure on Capella's fourth planet: a miserable little world, incidentally; if anyone is planning a visit, take my advice, don't! At any rate, I had joined a mineral survey team which was making a swing through the back-country. One night we camped near a tribe of the natives: the Bidrachate Dendicaps as you're all aware . . . ?" He looked around the table. "No? Well, they're rather decent creatures, about five feet tall, with a heavy black fur. They have two little legs, and what's under the fur is anybody's guess. Be this as it may, after we set up camp, about thirty 'caps came to visit us. We passed out sulfur, which they relish like salt, and for a lark I started up my portable record-player, one of the little Duo-dexes, with long-play slugs. A sturdy little instrument, not too long on tone—but one can't have everything. I tell you, the 'caps sat absolutely entranced. They stared at the little box for three hours, not moving a muscle. They even ignored their sulfur." And Bickel smiled at the recollection. From up and down the table came murmurs of amuse-ment. Lillian Monteagle said, "It's rather touching, really! Probably the first good music they had ever heard!"

Someone asked, "Did these—er, 'caps show any—well, call it understanding, or appreciation?"

Bernard Bickel; laughed. "Let me put it this way. I'm sure they missed the point of the Brandenburg Concertos. But they listened with the same attention that they gave the Nutcracker Suite, so at least we cannot accuse them of superficiality."

Dame Isabel frowned. "I'm not sure that I completely understand. You acknowledge the universality of music?"

"Oh—to some extent, if certain conditions are satisfied. Music is a communication—emotional communication, to be sure—and this implies agreement as to the context of the symbology. Do you follow me?"

"Naturally," snapped Dame Isabel. "I am Secretary-Treasurer of the Opera League; if I knew nothing of music I would hardly be allowed to continue in this capacity."

"Indeed? I was not aware of your——let us say—near-professional status."

Dame Isabel nodded crisply.

Bickel continued. "The point I wish to make is this. Musical symbology is at once simple and complex. A slow soft rhythmical sound is almost universally soothing. A series of shrill brassy staccato tones is likewise exciting. Abstraction on the first level. When we consider chords, chord progressions, tone clusters, melodic structure, then we deal with entities whose symbolic meaning is to a much greater degree a matter of convention. Even among the various musics of Earth there is no consensus as to the sig-nificance of these conventions. We can, if you like, speculate as to a possible congruence of musical symbology among the worlds of the galaxy. It is conceivable, through processes of acculturation, or parallel development—" he held up a hand as someone started to laugh "—don't be too skeptical too soon! The diatonic scale is not a freak, or a chance discovery! It is based on fundamental harmonic relationships. To exemplify: start with any note at random. For simplicity's sake C, which we will use as our base tone: the tonic. Even a child's ear can hear that another C an octave up or down the scale is the most obvious concord. A vibrational relationship of 2:1. Almost as basic will seem a concord with the vibration ratio 3:2. The note turns out to be G, the so-called dominant. What note occupies the same pragmatic relation to G that G does to C? It turns out to be the note we call D. With D as the tonic A becomes the dominant. With A as the tonic E is the dominant. Twelve different notes reveal themselves in this way before suddenly we find ourselves back at a note which is very close to C. Shift all these notes into the same octave, tinker and temper a little, and we have our familiar diatonic scale. Nothing mysterious, the most basic rule-of-thumb procedure imaginable. What is the point of all this? Simply that it should be no surprise to find a totally strange race on a totally strange planet using instruments similar to our own, employing our own familiar *do re me fa sol la ti do*."

"Ha, ha!" cried Dame Isabel. "This of course is what I have been telling stupid folk who cavil at Adolph Gondar and the Ninth Company!"

Bernard Bickel smilingly shook his head. "A different matter entirely! Agreed that the diatonic scale is a universal tool, like hinges, or the bowline, or the Pythagorean Theorem, the case of the evasive Adolph Gondar is something else again. No—" he held up a remonstrative hand "—do not accuse me of inconsistency. I merely find it hard to believe that the musical symbols and conventions of an alien race—as this 'Ninth Company of Rlaru' purports to be—could mesh so neatly and completely with our own as to affect us emotionally. Is this not reasonable?"

"Very reasonable," said Dame Isabel. "So reasonable as to indicate a flagrant fallacy in your chain of logic. The facts are these. I personally have sponsored Mr. Gondar. I am in full financial control of the tour, and I am not a woman to be fooled."

Bernard Bickel laughed. "In that case, I must review my thinking and seek out my 'flagrant fallacy.'"

"I suggest that you attend a performance," said Dame Isabel. "You may, if you like, join me in my box at tomorrow's performance."

Bernard Bickel said gravely, "I shall look into my appointments, and if at all possible, I shall do so."

* * * * * * *

But Bernard Bickel was never to enjoy a performance of the Ninth Company of Rlaru from Dame Isabel's luxurious box. During the night the entire Ninth Company vanished—completely, without trace or clue, as if they had dissolved into thin air.

Chapter Two

ROGER WOOL, after flying Dame Isabel to her beautiful old home Ballew, overlooking Ballew Valley, had elected to spend the night, rather than return to his apartment in the city. Hence he was present when Holker the butler placed the visiphone on the breakfast table with a murmured: "Mr. Gondar, madame. An urgent message."

"Thank you, Holker." Dame Isabel pushed down the key, and Gondar's face appeared on the screen. His eyes were more brooding than ever; his expression was remote, with no trace of the exuberance to be expected of an impresario.

"Well, Adolph?" inquired Dame Isabel. "What is the trouble?"

"It's simple enough," said Gondar. "The Ninth Company has disappeared."

"Disappeared, you say." Dame Isabel gave Gondar a long thoughtful glance; and Roger reflected that Bernard Bickel's remarks had possibly carried more weight than Dame Isabel had allowed. "Exactly what are the circumstances?"

"After last night's performance I escorted the troupe up to the theater penthouse. They fed themselves and seemed comfortably settled for the night—although I must say they all seemed rather excited—almost mischievous. I'd promised them an excursion—a sail on Mr. Saverino's yacht—and I assumed that this was behind their excitement . . . this morning—they just weren't there. The porter had allowed no one to leave by the street exit, the deck attendant swears no air vehicles arrived or departed."

"This is a serious business," said Dame Isabel. "One in which my personal reputation is involved. I must say that I am not completely satisfied."

"You're not?" growled Gondar. "Why shouldn't you be? You've got every cent we've made over the last three months. You've no cause for complaint."

"It appears that my precautions were absolutely in order. As you know, there has been a certain amount of cynical speculation regarding the authenticity of the troupe. I have always ignored it, but now I am forced to wonder exactly why, and exactly how, the troupe disappeared."

Gondar's dour expression never changed. "I will be happy to end our association," he said. "You need merely turn over to me my money."

"I will do nothing of the sort," said Dame Isabel. "I insisted on the arrangement for just this reason: that if ever there were a suggestion of fraud or trickery, I would be in a position to refund all money involved. As of now, I am not satisfied. You have told me very little of the planet Rlaru, and before I release any funds I must be absolutely sure of my position."

Gondar gave a grudging nod. "Will you be home this morning?"

"In the face of an emergency like this, naturally."

"I'll be there in half an hour." The visiphone went dark. Dame Isabel turned to Roger with a snort of dissatisfaction. "Sometimes it seems that all the world is false and coarse."

Roger rose to his feet. "Since I have an—"

"Sit down, Roger. I will need you here."

Roger resumed his seat.

Adolph Gondar was presently announced by Holker. He wore a somber suit of dark blue with white piping and scarlet gores at the waist, a loose dark blue cap with a spaceman's emblem. He carried a small case which he set to the side.

"Will you take coffee?" asked Dame Isabel. "Or do you prefer tea?"

"Neither," said Gondar. He looked at Roger, then

strode forward, to stand across the table from Dame Isabel, who this morning wore a handsome robe of lace and blue satin. "Sit down, Mr. Gondar, if you please."

Gondar drew forward a chair. "I feel," said Gondar, "that I should have my money. I have performed according to the terms of our—"

Dame Isabel said, "This is what I wish to determine. Our agreement includes a guarantee against 'misrepresentation, inaccuracy or suppression of fact.' I have meticulously observed these conditions—"

"And so have I!"

"Complete frankness has not existed. You have practised a studious secretiveness, and withheld so much significant fact that I consider our agreement vitiated."

Gondar recoiled in shock. "What do you mean by that?"

"I mean that our agreement is void. I refuse to release the money which has been earned by the troupe."

Gondar's face became pale and set. "I told you nothing but exact fact."

"But have you told me everything? Exactly how and where did you recruit the Ninth Company? Why did they disappear? Where are they now?"

Gondar chose to answer the last question. "In my opinion they've returned home."

"To Rlaru?" Dame Isabel's tone was skeptical.

"Yes. How I don't know. These people are adept in all sorts of techniques and sciences we know nothing about. I think they just decided to go home and went."

"By some psychic process, I presume?" Dame Isabel's voice dripped scorn.

"I wish I knew. I'd use it myself. On Rlaru I've seen things that I can't describe—musical productions which are absolutely overwhelming. Operas, I suppose you'd call them."

Dame Isabel's interest was aroused. "What sort of operas? Like those of the Ninth Company?"

"Oh no. The Ninth Company is a—well, not exactly a

comic troupe, but their repertory is what we would call light."

"Hmmf." Dame Isabel gazed out the window for a moment or two. "What inducements did you offer the Ninth Company to persuade them to visit Earth?"

Gondar in his turn became thoughtful. "I was on Rlaru for about four months. I learned something of the language. When I saw the quality of the performances, I mentioned that on Earth we had similar activities, and that perhaps we could effect a cultural exchange program." Roger started to laugh, then noticing both Dame Isabel's glance and Gondar's look of lambent displeasure he quickly quelled the sound. "No difficulties were made," Gondar went on. "I brought the Ninth Company to Earth, and in due course proposed to take an Earth group to Rlaru. But now—" he held out his hands "—nothing. I am mystified."

From a silver urn Dame Isabel absently poured a cup of coffee which she handed to Gondar. "You can find the planet Rlaru once more?"

"If necessary."

Dame Isabel frowned. "There is a disturbing quality to this situation, and it is to our mutual interest to discourage rumors. The company could not have gone off somewhere without notifying you?"

Gondar shook his head. "In my opinion they have returned to Rlaru, by some means beyond my knowledge."

"There is a highly developed science on the planet?"

"I wouldn't say that. Things aren't quite that simple—in fact it's a different situation completely. No one seems to work too hard, except maybe the lowest classes."

"Oh? This is a stratified society then?"

"I guess you'd call it that. At the top are aristocrats, who are also the musicians and pantomimists. Beneath is a kind of middle-class, which also has its artists and musicians. At the bottom is a caste of vagrants, no-talent indigents. If there are any scientists or production plants I didn't see any."

"You did not explore very thoroughly?"

"No. I was given to understand that it wasn't, well, safe, to go everywhere. No one told me why."

"Well, well. This is highly interesting. Certainly contact between the two planets must be continued. Roger, what is your opinion?"

"I agree, absolutely. No question whatever."

"The Opera League is meeting tonight," said Dame Isabel. "I shall report what you have told me, and recommend the cultural exchange program be kept up."

"All very well," said Adolph Gondar hollowly, "but what of my money?"

"In due course," said Dame Isabel. "It is safe and is accumulating interest. Furthermore, you have been remiss—very remiss indeed."

Gondar seemed puzzled. "How so?"

"You said nothing of our obligation to send a musical group to Rlaru. This is a business which cannot be handled in a half-hearted or slap-dash manner."

Gondar rubbed his long chin dubiously. He glanced sidewise at Roger, then returned to Dame Isabel. "I'm not so sure that it's a feasible project—in fact, now that I think of it . . ."

Dame Isabel's gaze became stony. "Mr. Gondar, I am never ambiguous nor untruthful, and I demand that everyone I deal with act in a similar manner. You made the assertion that the Ninth Company of Rlaru came to Earth as half of a cultural exchange scheme."

"Yes, of course, but——"

"Is this statement true or is it untrue?"

"Naturally it's true. However—"

"If it is true, the obligation is definite. Also—and you will certainly concur, for your reputation is as much under attack as mine—those persons who are attacking our good faith must be refuted. Do you not agree?"

"Yes. Yes, I agree. Definitely."

"We can serve both these ends by arranging a visit to Rlaru by a group of representative musicians."

Gondar gave a sour wince. "For reasons of my own I do not care to leave Earth. Not at the present time."

"Then I can only turn the money I control over to some worthy charity. In no other way can I demonstrate our integrity."

Gondar thought with great concentration, then heaved a long sigh of resignation. "Very well. Organize your tour. There can be no harm in it."

"Good. I am sure that the Opera League will enthusiastically support the project."

* * * * * *

Dame Isabel was mistaken. To her amazement the directors of the Opera League refused any sort of sponsorship to the project. "We have our dignity to consider," said Stillman Cordwainer, the Chairman. "I have it on reliable authority that Adolph Gondar is a mountebank. In my opinion we should repudiate him completely, and in the future use more caution."

"I agree in every respect," declared Bruno Brunofsky. "Next we'll be asked to sponsor a troupe of dancing bears."

Dame Isabel spoke in her iciest voice. "It is clear that the Directors have decided to scamp their responsibilities. I consider the policy of the Board insipid, sterile, callous and stupid; I have no choice but to tender my resignation, effective as of this instant. I myself shall undertake responsibility for this tour to Rlaru. If you will elect a new Secretary-Treasurer, I will turn over all my documents and accounts."

Chapter Three

WHEN ROGER WOOL read of his aunt's plans in the morning newspaper, his first emotion was astonishment; his second, dismay; his third, a blind instinctive urgency to act before it was too late.

Holker answered his visiphone call and placed him in contact with his aunt who sat at her escritoire looking through programs and memoranda. In a falsely jocular voice Roger called out, "Aunt Isabel have you seen the papers? They've published the most ridiculous report!"

"Oh?" Dame Isabel hardly looked up from her work. "We must have Biancolleli. And Otto von Scheerup." Then to Roger: "Yes, what were you saying?"

"The newspapers," said Roger. "They've printed the fantastic rumor that you're going off on a musical tour of space—something completely foolish. I really think you should sue, on grounds of—of—"

"Of what, Roger?"

"Scurrilous defamation—holding up to public ridicule."

"Roger, please stop sputtering. The articles are accurate in every respect. I indeed plan to organize an opera company and take it to Rlaru."

"But—think! The expense, the difficulties! There must be at least fifty people in an opera company—"

"I believe that we can do nicely with seventy-two or seventy-three. The company must necesarily be versatile, with all ancillary personnel willing and able to take minor parts."

17

"But a whole space-ship would be required: a crew, supplies—"

"I have interested my friend Admiral Rathelaw in the project; he will provide a suitable ship at realistic charter rates. This is the least of the difficulties."

"But you can't just go barging off into space like that! Think of the danger!"

"Nonsense. Mr. Bickel encountered the most cordial reception everywhere. You read far too many sensational novels, Roger; you obviously need an outlet for your energies: perhaps a job."

"Seriously," said Roger, "you have no idea of the problems, the detail, the headaches—"

"I will naturally hire competent persons to deal with these matters."

"But the expenses! Such a venture will cost millions!"

Dame Isabel shrugged. "I have ample means. When I am dead, what good is my money to me?"

Roger could not argue otherwise. As his aunt's closest relative, he presumed himself her heir, and the money she planned to squander on this extravagant expedition in a certain large sense was his own.

"We might even find ourselves turning a profit," said Dame Isabel cheerfully. "I certainly do not plan to confine our performances to Rlaru. I have strong convictions regarding the universality of music, and Mr. Bickel's description of the furry creatures listening to his record-player moved me deeply."

Roger started to speak, then thought better of it.

"My ideas are long-range," Dame Isabel went on. "We all recognize that the folk of the far planets often lack our musical perceptions; nevertheless any start we can make, any spark we can strike, may eventually lead to the most dramatic musical events: was it not Mr. Bickel himself who suggested that from just such people may come the powerful new musics of the future?"

"I thought you considered Mr. Bickel's opinions superficial," said Roger wearily.

"Everyone is entitled to his own point of view. Mr.

Bickel speaks at least with the authority of wide research, whereas gentlemen like Mr. Thorpe and Mr. Seaboro have learned all they know by listening to each other."

Roger made a disgruntled sound. "I certainly wouldn't put any faith in Adolph Gondar. What, after all, do you know of him?"

"I know that he must cooperate with me or never touch a penny of his earnings. And while we are on the subject of earning, it is high time that you settled into some sort of career. Yesterday I was called upon to settle several of your accounts. I make you a liberal allowance and I find this extravagance inexplicable . . ."

Roger finally was able to end the conversation. Glumly he pondered the future. He was more or less inured to Dame Isabel's eccentricities, but this affair was more monumental, more thorough-going than mere eccentricity; it was—Roger dutifully expunged the word.

What of his own position: Work. A job. Trifling remuneration for hours of his valuable time. It might become a matter of absolute necessity; Dame Isabel might well spend everything she owned on this most grotesquely expensive of caprices . . . Roger thought of Bernard Bickel. If anyone could dissuade her, it would be he. Roger called Bernard Bickel's room at the Nomad Inn.

Bickel took the call. He would be pleased to receive Roger, and there was no more convenient time than immediately.

Roger rode an air-bus to the Nomad Inn. Bickel met him in the lobby, and suggested coffee in the nearby Starfarer Lounge.

Once settled, with coffee and a tray of cakes, Bickel turned an inquiring eye upon Roger.

"You probably know why I've come to see you," said Roger.

"My dear fellow, I haven't the foggiest notion."

"You haven't heard of my aunt's new scheme?"

Bickel shook his head. "I've been out of town. Something amusing, I hope?"

"'Amusing.'" Roger echoed the word bitterly. "She

wants to take a grand opera company to this planet Rlaru. She'll spend millions without batting an eye."

Bickel listened with an occasional nod of the head, a whimsical pucker of the mouth. "Your aunt exemplifies a type which sadly is almost extinct: the affluent amateur, the wealthy eccentric. An impressive woman—though I can't share her faith in Captain Gondar."

"It's appalling!" declared Roger. "He's talked her into a project which will cost an enormous amount of money! She wants to visit other worlds along the way—you yourself have influenced her, with your description of the Bidrachate Dendicaps listening to music from your recorder."

Bernard Bickel laughed incredulously. "But it's all so ridiculous! Those particular creatures were merely wondering how I had been able to confine so many insects—which locally produce loud shrill noises—into so small a box. Your aunt's concept—excuse me if I speak frankly—is idiotic. The Dendicaps wouldn't know a concerto from a punch in the nose."

Roger laughed shakily. "She's been strongly influenced by your remarks. I wonder—I don't know how to put this to you—but could you find some way to set my aunt straight on the facts of the case?"

Bernard Bickel frowned, touched his handsome silver mustache. "I would be happy to advise your aunt, of course, but I can't simply go barging out and belabor her with my opinions."

"I tell you what!" exclaimed Roger. "Come out to Ballew today as my guest. She'll be delighted to see you."

Bickel gave a slight shrug. "I don't have anything else on—and I'd be happy to see your aunt's estate."

"Good! We can leave at any time you like."

"Oh . . . Two o'clock?"

"Excellent. I'll pick you up in my air-car."

Shortly before three Roger and Bernard Bickel arrived at Ballew. Roger landed his air-car on the flight deck, and Grumiano, the old porter, came to wheel it away into the garage.

Bernard Bickel went to the balustrade, surveyed the grounds. "A magnificent place, absolutely baronial! It must be hundreds of years old!"

"Yes, it's a beautiful place. And I don't want to see it sold at auction . . . We'll probably find my aunt in the rose garden, or perhaps on the south terrace."

Dame Isabel in fact was sitting at a marble table on the south terrace, dictating letters into a recorder, while simultaneously placing calls into a visiphone. She gave the two of them a terse nod, apparently failing to recognize Bernard Bickel. "Sit down, Roger, I'll be with you in a moment. I've got Marzic Ipsigori on the connection and we're trying to arrive at terms. I believe he will be with us."

Roger and Bernard Bickel waited while Dame Isabel spoke with the celebrated baritone, who, so it eventuated, could not give Dame Isabel a definite answer until he reviewed his obligations for the coming year.

Dame Isabel switched off the instrument, swung around to face Roger and Bickel. "Well, Roger: who is your friend? But of course, it's Mr. Bickel."

"Yes, and delighted for the opportunity to see your home and its glorious grounds."

Dame Isabel nodded. "Ballew is at its best during the summer. Roger, find Holker and have him lay tea."

When Roger returned Dame Isabel and Bernard Bickel were strolling through the rose garden, talking with great animation. From time to time Dame Isabel laughed heartily, and Bernard Bickel also seemed to be enjoying himself. At least, thought Roger, his aunt was listening without resentment. Perhaps she herself had begun to have misgivings about the enormous complexity of the project. Roger sighed with gratification: taking his problems to Bernard Bickel had been a wise move.

Holker laid the table for tea; Dame Isabel and Bickel came to join Roger.

"Good news, Roger!" exclaimed Dame Isabel. "Good news indeed! Mr. Bickel has agreed to join our little tour among the planets! He'll be musical consultant, at a very exorbitant salary, I'm sorry to say—" she chuckled roguishly "—but we will have his specialized knowledge to guide us!"

Roger looked in shock and pain at Bernard Bickel, who nodded smilingly. "I will be utterly honest," said Bickel. "You could not have hired a better man. There are dozens of pitfalls into which, without expert counsel, you would have been sure to fall."

Roger rose; Dame Isabel looked up in surprise. "Roger: are you not staying for dinner?"

"No," said Roger. "I've just remembered an engagement." He bowed grimly to Bernard Bickel and took his leave.

Dame Isabel sighed. "Roger is beyond my comprehension. A dear fellow, but like so many of his generation, without direction. I've arranged a position for him with Atlantic Securities. The world of stocks and bonds is said to be fascinating, and I'm sure the challenge of regular hours will prove stimulating."

"Quite correct," said Bernard Bickel. "You've made a sensible decision."

Chapter Four

FROM A journalistic standpoint, the world at this particular juncture was torpid. No political contests were in progress; the Hall-Anderson Vituperation Trials had ended; the final restoration of ancient Athens was accomplished; no one had seen the Loch Ness Monster for several months. The divorce of Barbara Bankwiler from the Grand Duke of Tibet had been predictable; the new air-car models were still several months in the offing. Here and there, of course, was news of a sort; the Blue Man Society had purchased a million acre tract in central Mauretania, centered on the Sebkra de Chinchane, where vacationing members could enjoy the ancient nomadic existence; a hollow pretzel, containing thirteen fluid ounces of beer, had reached the market; the Gaudalajara Coyotes, Las Vegas Dodgers, Osaka Earthquakes, Saint Louis Browns, Milan Green Sox, and Bangalore Avatars were allowed about equal chances in the forthcoming World Series. But these were mere stirs in the summer doldrums, and Dame Isabel's projected tour of remote planets aroused world-wide interest. Experts were solicited for comment; their statements were probed and explored, until eventually a full scale controversy raged across the intellectual community. Spokesmen for one point of view bluntly labeled Dame Isabel a crackpot and the whole project a musical boondoggle; others remarked that the experience must—at the very least—be edifying for all concerned. In a persuasive article for the *Cosmologician* Bernard Bickel wrote: "It may well be that not every individual of every planet will fully appreciate the whole of the repertory—but there must be an impact of some sort: at worst, simple wonder for the sound and color; at best an enthusiastic, if perhaps intuitive, response (never forget, the basic offering will be classic grand opera, a mannered and sophisticated form of music). We may encounter races with elaborate sound-structures of their own; many exist: I myself have encountered several. Other races are completely deaf, and to these music is unimaginable. Nevertheless, none of these people can fail to be impressed by the grandeur of classical grand opera and by the artistic energy of the people which have produced it. We shall achieve at the least good public relations; at the most we shall contribute a meaningful experience to races less fortunate than ourselves."

In another article Bernard Bickel cautiously touched on the planet Rlaru: "Unluckily I missed all but a brief moment of the performances of the Ninth Company. I must say that this *soupçon* gave me food for thought. As to the whereabouts of Rlaru, I cannot say: even the most peripatetic of musicologists can visit but a small fraction of the inhabited worlds. One point I would like to make, which seems not to have been touched on before: the Ninth Company, according to all reports, consisted of individuals both more and less than human, but nonetheless members of the cosmologically numerous anthropoid type. If features, anatomy and configuration can demonstrate parallel evolution, why is not the same possible for musical idiom—especially since harmonics is as objective a science as chemistry?

"Temporarily let us put the whole question into abeyance. Providence and Adolph Gondar concurring we will visit this wonder planet and, we shall see for ourselves. If matters are as purported—or if they are not—we shall return with specific information. Until then I advise all to withhold judgment."

* * * * * *

Roger had accepted employment with Atlantic Securities, for he knew better than to make difficulties: it was always wise to bend with the blast. Sure enough, events worked out as he had expected. After a week of amiable botchery, he was called before Mr. McNab to be told that certain alarming financial trends had made retrenchment necessary. Mr. Wool, the most recent employee, must be the first to go.

Roger, putting on a lugubrious air, went out to Ballew to explain the matter to his aunt, only to learn that she had gone to the space-port in the company of Bernard Bickel. Roger followed, and found Dame Isabel at the fitting-out dock to the north of the field. Here the *Phoebus* (so Dame Isabel had named the ship) was being converted to the special uses for which she intended it.

The *Phoebus*, Roger found as he circled it seeking Dame Isabel, was a large ship, consisting of five globes sixty feet in diameter joined by ovoidal tubes twenty feet across the largest dimensions. One globe had been opened and altered to form a stage, and here Roger found Dame Isabel, consulting with the project engineer. She greeted Roger briefly, and, so it seemed, with neither surprise nor disapproval.

Roger drew a few cautious breaths, threw back his shoulders, and felt as if the worst was over, for on similar occasions in the past Dame Isabel had exhibited a brassy volubility. Now she listened attentively as the engineer described the manner in which he had fitted the stage into the ship. The pentagonal shape of the *Phoebus* enclosed an appreciable area; at its center a stanchion could be erected, cables strung to each of the globes, and all covered with a light fabric to form a tent-like auditorium.

Bernard Bickel joined the group. He had been off inspecting the living accomodations and now reported all in order. Dame Isabel's cabin seemed a trifle cramped, he remarked, as perhaps did his own cabin and office. Could not both be expanded at least in some small degree? The engineer agreed to look into the matter.

Dame Isabel's attention wandered. Her eye fell on Roger; her face changed. "Roger! What on earth are you doing here? Why aren't you at your position?"

Roger was caught unaware. "A temporary lay-off," he stammered, "or so I hope. The market is extremely slow; Mr. McNab tells me there's going to be a big shakedown in the business, and he's had to put about a third of his staff on call."

"Indeed?" said Dame Isabel frostily. "He said nothing of this when I spoke to him."

Roger stated that in the financial world disaster often struck with the speed of a lightning bolt. "Mr. McNab naturally wanted to keep me on, but he said that everyone else would consider it favoritism. I told him not to consider my feelings, but do what he thought best."

"Roger," said Dame Isabel, "I simply don't know what to do with you. You have an excellent education, good manners, a certain vapid charm which you employ when it suits you, and an undeniable talent for high living. What would you do without your allowance from me? Would you starve? Or do you think the demands of your stomach might bring you to grips with reality?"

Roger accepted the dressing-down with what he felt to be remarkable dignity. Eventually Dame Isabel threw up her hands. "I suppose that so long as I have a crust I must share with you." She gave her attention once more to the engineer, and Roger turned away with relief.

Now he noticed an extremely attractive girl inspecting the *Phoebus*. She wore a brown suit with black piping, a brown and black toque: she was a trifle taller than average, with the easy carriage of unself-conscious health. Her hair was brown, her eyes were hazel-brown, her features were perfectly ordered. Roger's first impression was favorable, together with his second and third. The girl radiated female magnetism; to look at her was to want to approach her, touch her, establish proprietary rights. But there was more to the girl than physical charm. Even at first glance—and Roger had never before considered himself intuitive—he sensed in her something miraculous and extraordinary, a legendary *élan* which could not be defined.

The girl noticed Roger's attention. She did not seem disturbed. Roger smiled, though without any great fervor: the recent dressing-down had not tended to exalt his self-esteem. But the girl examined him with an expression which was almost admiration; and Roger wondered if by some magic this gloriously beautiful girl had seen deep inside him, had grasped the magnificent essence of his true self.

Now—wonder of wonders!—she approached him; she spoke: her voice was soft, with a half-heard lilt Roger could not identify, which gave her every utterance the pulse of poetry. "That lady over there—is she Dame Isabel Grayce?"

"Yes indeed; you are absolutely correct," said Roger. "You couldn't be more so."

"And who is that man talking to her?"

Roger looked over his shoulder. "That's Mr. Bickel. A musical expert, or so he fancies himself."

"And you are a musician?"

Roger suddenly wished that such were the case; it was clear that this girl wanted him to be a musician, that she would have approved . . . Well, he could always learn. "Yes—in a way."

"Oh? Really?"

"Yes, indeed," said Roger. "I play the—well, I'm one of those all-around types . . . Er, who are you?"

The girl smiled. "That's a question I can't answer—because I'm not absolutely sure. But I'll tell you my name—if you'll tell me yours."

"I'm Roger Wool."

"You're associated with Dame Isabel Grayce?"

"She's my aunt."

"Indeed!" The girl gave him an admiring look. "And you're going on this expedition out among the planets?"

Until this instant Roger had never considered the possibility. He frowned, darted a cautious glance toward his aunt, and was startled to meet her gaze. Dame Isabel turned an appraising glance upon the girl, and Roger realized instantly that she did not approve. Dame Isabel liked hearty no-nonsense types, without hidden layers or dark shadows. This girl was layered and shadowed and full of a thousand shimmers. "Yes," said Roger. "I think I'll probably be going along. It seems like fun."

She nodded solemnly, as if Roger had enunciated a cosmic truth "I'd like to travel space too."

"You haven't told me your name," said Roger.

"So I haven't. It's a strange name, or so I'm told."

Roger was beside himself with impatience. "Tell me."

Her lips twitched. "Madoc Roswyn."

Roger asked her to spell it, and she did so. "Actually, it's a Welsh name, from Merioneth, to the west of the Berwyn Mountains, though now there's none of us left: I'm the last."

Roger wanted to console her, but Dame Isabel was approaching with short sharp steps. "Roger, who is your friend?"

"Dame Isabel Grayce, Miss Madoc Roswyn."

Dame Isabel gave a curt nod. Madoc Roswyn said, "I am grateful for the privilege of meeting you, Dame Isabel. I think you are doing a wonderful thing, and I would like to join you."

"Indeed," Dame Isabel's glance raked Madoc Roswyn from head to toe. "You perform?"

"Never professionally. I sing, I play the piano, and the concertina, and also some rather silly instruments like the tin whistle."

Dame Isabel replied in the driest of voices. "Unfortunately our repertory will be almost entirely classical grand opera, though I expect to include one or two of the Early Decadents."

"Mightn't there be intermission numbers, or an occasional light program? I'm very adaptable, and I'm sure I could make myself useful in dozens of ways."

"This may well be true," said Dame Isabel. "Unfortunately space is at a premium. If you were a soprano of the highest quality, absolutely secure in the principal Russian, French, Italian and German works, I would be disposed to offer you an audition, together with six other sopranos who fit the requirements. The company must function like a smoothly-working machine, with every element contributing to the whole. Unrelated pieces, such as concertinas and tin whistles, would be quite redundant."

Madoc Roswyn smiled politely. "I must accept your decision, of course. But if ever you consider a slighter, more informal program, I hope you will think of me."

"I can promise you this much, certainly. Presumably Roger can get in touch with you."

"Yes, of course. Thank you for your attention, and I wish you great success."

Dame Isabel turned away. She called back over her shoulder. "I shall expect you at Ballew this evening, Roger. We must come to certain decisions."

Roger, suddenly bold, took Madoc Roswyn's arm, and the contact tingled nerves all the way up his arm. "I know what," he said. "I'll take you to lunch, and between courses you can play the tin whistle."

"I wish I'd brought it."

Roger led her to the little sky-car; away they flew to a mountain-top inn, and Roger had never had a more enchanting lunch. He made dozens of extravagant statements, which Madoc Roswyn heard with exactly the right mixture of amusement, skepticism and tolerance. Roger tried to find out all about her: he wanted, in one brief hour, to make up for a lifetime of non-acquaintance, a lifetime for all practical purposes wasted. Madoc Roswyn's background, as she explained it, was simple and uncomplicated. Her family had been landholders and farmers in a rather remote area of Wales; she had attended school in a little stone village, and secondary school at Llangollen. When her parents died she had sold the old farmstead, and since had traveled the world. She had worked at one job here, another there, uncertain what to do with herself, but disinclined to compromise her freedom. It came to Roger that here, exactly, was his own predicament: he was neither lazy or incompetent; he merely had occupational claustrophobia. As for Madoc Roswyn and all her candor there was still mystery: areas and areas behind areas: quirks of emotions he could never divide; goals and dedications of which she would never hint.

The realization was painful: no matter how much he had of her, there would always be more forever beyond his reach . . . His first enthusiasm muted, Roger conveyed Madoc Roswyn to her lodgings. He would have liked to have taken her to Ballew for the evening, but somehow did not dare.

*   *   *   *   *   *

At dinner Dame Isabel pointedly made no mention of Madoc Roswyn. Bernard Bickel was present and conversation centered upon the formation of the company. "I insist upon Guido Altrochi," said Dame Isabel. "I could get Nels Lessing, in fact he's offered to join the company without pay and Guido wants a frightful salary—but I refuse to compromise. Only the best is good enough."

Bernard Bickel nodded approvingly. "If only there were more like you!"

Roger winced. "If I were handling the matter," he said, "I'd use three-dimension records. Why not? Think how much easier, and how much less expensive!"

Dame Isabel shook her head. "Canned performances are always deficient, they never convey the vitality, the living, breathing, presence of music."

"Good enough for the back-planets," growled Roger.

"We are sufficiently at the mercy of machines, Roger; if our music must necessarily be mechanical, then it is time for us to throw in the sponge, and abandon all hope for the future of humanity."

"Assuming that opera is music in the first place," muttered Roger.

"I beg your pardon?"

"I merely emphasized the enormous savings to be achieved."

"Someday, my young friend," said Bernard Bickel, "you will appreciate your aunt's wisdom and courage. What are a few paltry dollars? Nothing less than the physical presence of the artists, working in perfect discipline, can generate the excitement of a legitimate musical experience—and it is this excitement, this sense of wonder, which we want to convey!"

Roger could summon further arguments, and listened while Dame Isabel and Bernard Bickel debated the merits of Cassandra Prouty against those of Nellie Mlanova; weighed Ruger Mandelbaum's undeniable stage sense against his corpulence which unfitted him for certain roles. Blitza Soerner was weak in Italian, but no one alive better understood the Decadents. Bernard Bickel nominated Andrei Szinc for the position of stage director. Dame Isabel concurred. And so on for two hours, while Roger traced circles on the tablecloth with his spoon.

"Regarding one choice there can be no argument," declared Dame Isabel. "Our conductor must be Sir Henry Rixon! It would be impossible to proceed without him."

Roger looked up from the tablecloth, wondering if by some means he could spirit Sir Henry Rixon away for six months, until his aunt lost interest in this fantastically expensive junket.

Bernard Bickel frowned thoughtfully. "Sir Henry Rixon—or Siebert Holgeness."

"Of course! I neglected him," admitted Dame Isabel, "and there's that marvellous young Jarvis Akers." Roger returned his attention to the tablecloth. Sir Henry Rixon he might contrive to imprison on a remote island, but hardly half a dozen others.

Dame Isabel finally looked around at Roger. "And now, Roger, what in the world will we do with you?"

"Well," said Roger, "I'm almost inclined to make the trip with the *Phoebus*."

Dame Isabel gave her head a curt shake. "Impossible, Roger. Space is at a premium, as I told your friend Miss Roswyn today."

Roger had expected no more. "I think you should at least give Miss Roswyn an audition. She's highly talented."

"Doubtless. Just who is this young woman, Roger? What is your connection with her?"

"No connection whatever. I just happened to know she is musically competent and—"

"Please, Roger, do not talk of what you do not understand."

* * * * * *

The following day Roger once again lunched with Madoc Roswyn. She seemed to enjoy his company and as they left the restaurant she slipped her hand into his.

In his air-car they flew out over the ocean. Roger said abruptly, "I've only known you two days, but I feel as if it's been—well, to be honest, two days."

Madoc Roswyn laughed. "I like you, Roger. You're so relaxing. So undemanding . . . I'll miss you when you're gone."

Roger swallowed hard, and made a gallant sacrifice. "The hell with the space-tour. I'd rather stay with you. In fact—let's get married!"

Madoc Roswyn sadly shook her head. "If you missed this marvelous expedition on my account, you'd start resenting me. Not right away perhaps—but you'd get restless, and presently you'd grow to hate me. I've seen it happen to other people . . . I'll never stand in your way. You go with the tour, and I'll keep on as before."

"If only Aunt Isabel wasn't such an obdurate old creature!" exclaimed Roger. "We could both go!"

"Oh Roger! Wouldn't that be wonderful! But it won't happen."

"It can! And it will! Just leave it to me!"

"Oh Roger—I'm so excited!" She threw her arms around Roger's neck and kissed him. Roger put the air-car on automatic, but Madoc Roswyn moved across the seat. "Roger, behave yourself. You're the most hot-blooded thing. . ."

"You will marry me?"

Madoc Roswyn considered with wryly pursed mouth. "Not if we're going to be separated right away."

Roger flung his arms in the air. "What's a little space-trip? I'll stay home!"

"Now, Roger, we've been all over this before."

"True. I forgot. Then we'll both make the trip on the *Phoebus*."

Madoc Roswyn smiled wistfully. "Your aunt was fairly definite in this regard."

"Leave it to me," said Roger. "I know just how to handle the old crock."

* * * * * *

Dame Isabel was in a good mood. Sir Henry Rixon, Andrei Szinc, and Ephraim Zerner, the great Wagnerian basso, had all agreed to join the *Phoebus* company, and there should now be no trouble enlisting other musicians of equal prestige.

Roger listened from the side of the room as Sir Henry outlined his thoughts on the orchestra. "We'll be forced to compromise here and there, but it's naturally absurd to contemplate a hundred and twenty piece orchestra. And, as you know, I consider the smaller orchestra more versatile, and capable of more bite. So with your approval, I will select instrumentalists on this basis."

Sir Henry Rixon shortly departed; Dame Isabel sat musing a moment then rang the bell for tea. She turned to Roger. "Well? What did you think of Sir Henry?"

"Very impressive," said Roger. "The best possible man for the position."

Dame Isabel gave a dry chuckle. "I am happy to hear your approval."

"Yes, I'm looking forward to the trip."

Holker wheeled in the tea service; Dame Isabel poured two cups of tea with two decisive motions. "As I said before, Roger, I have no intention of taking you along. You would only be so much dead weight."

"I don't see why I shouldn't get some enjoyment out of the trip," growled Roger. "All the parasites you've hired are complacent enough."

"Please do not call these people parasites, Roger; they are musicians."

"Parasites, musicians—it amounts to the same thing. The back-planet people won't know the difference."

"No?" asked Dame Isabel with dangerous softness.

"Of course not. The whole project is batty. These creatures are completely alien to us; how in the name of the Seven Muses can they appreciate music of any sort, let alone grand opera? My advice is: call the affair off and save no end of money!"

Once more Dame Isabel gave her wintry chuckle. "At times, Roger, you become absolutely florid in your rhetoric. I am particularly impressed by your evocation of the Muses. But in your solicitude for my pocketbook you neglect certain facts. For instance, how do you explain the enormous success of the Ninth Company here on Earth?"

Roger sipped his tea. "Well—they were almost human."

Dame Isabel said placidly, "There are hundreds of man-like races among the peoples of the galaxy."

Roger remembered his primary purpose. After a frowning study of his tea-cup he nodded slowly. "Well—you may be right. No doubt the trip will be interesting, and certainly someone should keep an accurate day-by-day journal." Roger looked up as if struck by a sudden inspiration. "This is a job I'd like to take on myself. Eventually we could publish the journal as a documentary record of the trip. With photographs, soundstrips . . . You could write a forward . . ."

Dame Isabel started to speak, then stopped. Finally she said, "You believe you have the capacity to undertake a work of this sort?"

"Of course! Writing is the profession for which I'm best suited."

Dame Isabel sighed. "Very well, Roger. I see that you're determined to accompany the tour, and I suppose I must allow it."

"Thank you, Aunt Isabel."

"I suggest that you learn something of the history and development of grand operas, and try to cultivate at least a modicum of taste. You would feel foolish indeed if a native of a distant world showed a deeper feeling for our music than you did yourself."

"No fear of that," said Roger, and Dame Isabel looked at him sharply, suspecting a possible ambiguity.

"Perhaps I'd better look over the projected itinerary," said Roger, "so that I can make a start on research."

Dame Isabel silently handed him a sheet of paper, which Roger studied a moment or two. He looked up with an expression of rueful wonder. "Some of these worlds are barely explored!"

"Our itinerary," said Dame Isabel, "is necessarily determined by the location of planets where we can expect a hospitable and appreciative audience. You see, Roger, that contrary to your beliefs, we are neither irresponsible nor impractical; we do not plan to perform *Die Walküre* before a colony of floating polyps or the like. Give us at least this much credit."

"Oh indeed." Roger studied the list. "And which of these worlds is the highly-advertised Rlaru?"

"Please restrain your sarcasm, Roger; your connection with the tour is still at best tentative. As for Rlaru, Captain Gondar will guide us there at the appropriate time. He has sound reasons for keeping his own counsel until after the *Phoebus* leaves Earth."

"Maybe, maybe not," grumbled Roger. "If I were you, I'd get some sort of guarantee that this Gandor fellow won't maroon us all out back of beyond—and that's not sarcasm, but plain common-sense."

Dame Isabel's patience was wearing thin. "I have every faith in Captain Gondar. In addition, I control a very large sum of money which ultimately he will receive. And in the third place if you fear so absurd a contingency, you need not accompany the tour."

"My concern is only for yourself and the tour," protested Roger. "Naturally I'm looking out for every possible source of trouble."

"I have already done so. Now, if you will excuse me, I have some correspondence to take care of, and I must shuffle accommodations to make room for you."

"Oh I won't require much room," said Roger bluffly. "My secretary can work in Bickel's office, which he won't need anyway, and as for sleeping arrangements—well, just bunk us in anywhere."

Dame Isabel stared at Roger in astonishment. "What on earth are you talking about? If by 'secretary' you refer to that extremely subtle young woman I met at the spaceport, you had better change your ideas decisively."

"She is an accomplished secretary," said Roger sulkily, "and in addition she is my fiancée."

Dame Isabel made a set of fretful motions, as if troubled by her inability to express the inexpressible. Finally she said, "You fail to grasp a fundamental fact. This is a serious expedition, undertaken by persons dedicated to an artistic idea, and by no means an amorous idyll."

Later that evening Roger called Madoc Roswyn by visiphone. At his news her delightful mouth dropped sadly. "Oh Roger, what a shame. Do you think she'll change her mind?"

"Not a chance. For some reason she's taken a—well, not exactly aversion—"

Madoc Roswyn nodded. "Women never seem to like me. Why, I don't know. I never flirt or attract attention—"

"It's because you're so utterly beautiful," said Roger. "How you could ever agree to marry such an ordinary man as myself I'll never understand."

"I don't know what I'll do while you're gone," sighed Madoc Roswyn. "Perhaps I'll go to live in Paris; I have some friends there; I'd never be lonely."

"I'll stay home from this idiotic expedition," raved Roger. I don't care if I—"

"No, Roger. It just wouldn't work."

"Then, by golly, you'll come along, if I have to stow you away!"

"Oh Roger! Would you dare?"

"Of course I'd dare! I'm the most daring hell-raising aunt-defier known to the humanoid universe, and if you don't believe me I'm coming over to your apartment and make you believe me."

"I believe you, Roger—but can we get away with it?"

"With what?"

"Stowing me away."

Roger hesitated. "You're serious?"

"Yes."

Roger took a deep breath. "Very well. So be it."

Chapter Five

THE *PHOEBUS* was two hours in space. The opera company and the musicians stood staring rather wistfully back toward Earth. Dame Isabel kept to her cabin, suffering, so the rumor went, from acute space-sickness: a report lent credence by the frequent comings and goings of Dr. Shand, the ship physician.

Adolph Gondar—now Captain Gondar—remained on the bridge with Logan de Appling, the personable young astrogator. Roger Wool was seen in several quarters of the ship. His pallor and extreme nervousness were ascribed to space-sickness. Bernard Bickel went here and there answering questions, calming nervous qualms and generally maintaining the morale of the company, while Sir Henry Rixon inspected the stowage of musical instruments, to make sure that the vibration of take-off had not damaged the two grand pianos.

The first meal of the voyage was presently announced: a necessarily informal repast served cafeteria style. The mess-steward, noticing Roger passing a second time before the trays, cried out jocularly, "Here's a man with a good appetite! Eat like this, you'll soon be fat!"

Roger flushed. "I happen to be hungry," he said rather shortly, and went off with the tray.

"Touchy chap," the mess-steward told George Jameson, the percussionist. "Hope there's not too many like him aboard."

"That's Dame Isabel's nephew," said Jameson. "She keeps him on a pretty short leash; no surprise if he's a bit peevish."

38

"I can't see where he stows all that grub," said the steward. "He doesn't have the look of a big eater."

At the next meal Roger's voracity was once again noted. "Look," said the bus-boy. "That chap is taking a tray out of the saloon! Do you think he's some kind of a food hoarder?"

The next meal or two Roger was circumspect, but it was not long before the mess-steward noticed Roger dropping morsels of food into a sack.

Two hours later an obsequious bus-boy informed Roger that Dame Isabel wished to speak to him at once.

With leaden steps Roger went to Dame Isabel's cabin. Her face, the color of oatmeal from the effects of space-sickness, was stern. "Sit down, Roger," she said. "I have several things to say to you. I preface them by a remark to the effect that of all human failings I find ingratitude among the most despicable. Do I make myself clear?"

"If you are speaking in a general sense, yes."

"To particularize, I allude to the presence of your 'fiancée' aboard the ship." She held up her hand. "Do not interrupt. I have in the past held you in affection, and when I ended my days I had planned to bequeath to you a not inconsiderable proportion of my estate. The disclosures of this last hour force me completely to alter my intentions. I will say no more, except that our first port of call is Sirius Planet, and there you and that woman will be put ashore.

"Aunt Isabel," cried Roger in anguish, "things are not the way you think they are! Let me explain!"

"The facts speak for themselves. Your paramour is in Captain Gondar's custody, and I believe he has improvised a brig in a storage locker. You are lucky that you are not treated likewise. And now leave me. It is a shame that together with this dreadful space-sickness I must be burdened with the impudicities of my nephew."

"One last remark," said Roger sternly. "She is not my paramour, she is my fiancée! And not for lack of trying either. But she has absolutely refused to let me more than kiss her cheek until we are married—which I hope will be

soon. Put us off at Sirius Planet if you so choose, but spare
me your hypocrisy; I have heard tales about you when you
were fifty years younger, and if they're true, Miss
Roswyn's stowing away is absolutely trivial."

"Get out of here, you impudent whelp," exclaimed
Dame Isabel, in the deep nasal hoarseness which signaled
her most vehement feelings.

Roger departed the cabin. Head hanging, he wandered
down the passageway. Disowned! Disinherited! In dis-
grace! He sighed. What matter? Madoc Roswyn's affection
was ample recompense. He went to the bridge to confer
with Captain Gondar and to his surprise found Madoc
Roswyn sitting quietly on a bench. She looked up as he entered, then looked down at her hands. She seemed so
helpless, so despairing, so forlorn, that Roger could barely
restrain himself from running across the room to console
her. But he turned to Captain Gondar, who in his dark
uniform seemed more brooding and saturnine than ever. "I
understand that my aunt has placed Miss Roswyn in your
custody."

"That is correct, Mr. Wool."

"Will you allow me to have a few private words with
her?"

Captain Gondar's reply came as something of a surprise
to Roger: "Haven't you done enough damage already?"
And Roger saw that the long spare face was taut and angry. Then Gondar shrugged. "If Miss Roswyn is willing to
talk with you, it's certainly agreeable to me."

Madoc Roswyn looked toward Captain Gondar with a
strange expression on her face, one which puzzled Roger;
it was almost as if she were pleading with him. Captain
Gondar made a quick harsh movement, turned away.
Madoc Roswyn arose, followed Roger into the corridor.
Roger attempted to take her in his arms, but she stepped
back. "Please, Mr. Wool—say what you want to say, and
then—"

"My darling!" gasped Roger. "What's wrong?"

" 'What wrong?' " she gave a bitter laugh. "The mess

you've got me in, the things you've said about me—it's a wonder I've a shred of reputation left!"

"I don't understand!" bleated Roger. "I've merely—"

"You've merely got me in the worst trouble I've ever been in! I'm thankful I know you for the selfish blunderer you are before you did worse than you've done! Now please go, and never speak to me again! Captain Gondar at least is decent enough to arrange me a place to sleep and see that I don't go hungry!"

Roger turned blindly away, and almost stumbled into Captain Gondar who had been standing in the doorway.

An hour later Captain Gondar presented himself to Dame Isabel. "Yes, Captain? How are things going?"

"Everything seems first-rate, madame. I've made arrangements in regard to the young lady whom I fear your nephew had attempted to victimize."

"What? Roger victimize anyone except me? Certainly not that devious little trollop."

Captain Gondar's face darkened. "Eventually you'll hear the full truth, madame. In the meantime the young lady is not only filled with remorse, but wants to make amends for the trouble she unwittingly has caused."

"You speak in riddles," snapped Dame Isabel. "How could she 'unwittingly' have done anything?"

"Mr. Wool tricked her aboard. She was drugged, and awoke to find herself locked in a storage closet. Mr. Wool made periodic attempts to assault her, but without success."

Dame Isabel emitted a hoarse caw of laughter. "If it's true—though I doubt it—it's about the level of competence I'd expect of Roger. He has a girl locked in a closet, drugged and helpless and still she fends him off. Well, well, well. Poor Roger."

"The young lady learned that you were suffering from space-sickness, and was quite concerned. She tells me that she knows a specific cure and will be happy to help you."

Dame Isabel rubbed her pallid forehead. "The way I feel, I'd take help from the devil himself. What is this cure?"

"I'll fetch her, and we'll see what she can do."

Madoc Roswyn came into the room. She looked at Dame Isabel a moment or two, nodded thoughtfully and spoke a few quiet words to Captain Gondar. He departed and Madoc Roswyn approached Dame Isabel. "Now, madame, if you'll relax and close your eyes, I'll try to stimulate the nerves which strange new conditions have cramped. Captain Gondar has gone for some medicine— an old farm recipe from the Welsh hills . . ." She touched Dame Isabel here and there, on throat, neck, forehead.

Captain Gondar returned with a glass, which proved to contain a thick turgid liquid. "What is that?" demanded Dame Isabel suspiciously.

"Sulfur, honey and a little drop of whiskey. Drink it and you'll feel a new woman."

Dame Isabel drank the potion, made a wry face. "It will be either cure or kill." Madoc Roswyn continued to touch her here and there, hardly more than glancing little flicks of the finger-tips. Dame Isabel sat up in her chair. In a voice of wonder she said, "Why, do you know, I *do* feel better!"

"I'm very pleased," said Madoc Roswyn and quietly departed.

"Hmph," said Dame Isabel. "She unquestionably has a way with her . . . Strange creature . . . Of course she must be put off at Sirius Planet. But in the meanwhile see that she's comfortable. I owe her at least that much. Hmmf. That lummox Roger. What in the world will become of him?"

* * * * * *

The *Phoebus*, encapsulated in non-stuff like a worm in an oak-gall, slid across space with the speed of thought. The sun became a star, with Sirius a brighter star dead ahead. The musicians occupied themselves with practice, the vocalists with exercises and rehearsals. There were the inevitable outbursts of temperament, the formation and dissolution of cliques, several romances, as many quarrels, a spate of gossip, innuendo and caustic comment, and by these activities the ravages of space-sickness were for the most part avoided.

At the halfway point Dame Isabel presided at a champagne party, where she made an address to the company: "I am very pleased by the manner in which everyone has adapted to the circumstances of the voyage. Ahead of us lies Sirius and Sirius Planet which for most of us will be a first venture upon an alien world. Sirius Planet is not at all like Earth except in gravity and atmosphere. It occupies what I believe is known as the 'Trojan position' in relation to Sirius A and Sirius B; and receives only a tenth of the radiation Earth receives from the sun. Nevertheless a comfortable temperature is maintained both by internal heat and a 'greenhouse' atmosphere, which very efficiently retains heat. There is flora and fauna unlike anything with which we are familiar, and in fact the words 'flora' and 'fauna' are probably misnomers, as many of the Sirius life-forms fit neither category, or fit them both. There is an intelligent native population, which of course is the reason for our visit. Mr. Bickel will tell us more about the autochthones in a moment. I will anticipate him only to say that this race is not musically oriented—in fact the style of the native civilization might at first glance seem rather primitive, for they live in caves and potholes. Still we must avoid parochialism; it is possible that the byzantaurs, as the race is called, regard us as equally primitive.

"I have given a good deal of thought to our first program. A choice is more difficult than you might suppose. It is necessary to maintain an exquisite balance. We want to communicate with our audience, but still hold our artistic integrity at its highest levels. To this end we must select works which offer the largest possible number of contacts with the audience's own milieu, the largest possible number of situations with which they can identify their own existences. I have decided that *Fidelio* will be our first offering, since much of the action occurs in a dungeon not unlike the blowholes in which the byzantaurs live.

"Now, Mr. Bickel will tell us something more of the byzantaurs and the circumstances of their life."

Bernard Bickel arose, bowed urbanely. He wore a casual garment of black silk, tight at the ankles and belt, with a smart gold and silver piping; his neat silver mustache was crisp as a wire brush. With a polite smile of self-deprecation, he said, "Dame Isabel has covered the ground quite thoroughly; but I can fill in one or two details regarding the byzantaurs and the nature of their existences, since I have had occasion to visit Sirius three—or has it been four?—times previously. In any event I know Commandant Boltzen at the settlement well, and look forward to renewing our acquaintance.

"As Dame Isabel has pointed out, Sirius Planet is a rather dim place, about as bright as an Earth twilight. One's eyes rapidly adapt to the dimness and the landscape takes on a weird charm. Sirius Settlement lies almost beneath the Trapezus Vulcanism, and nearby live the Royal Giant byzantaurs, probably the most civilized tribe of the planet. Like the landscape, I fear they will seem initially ugly to your eyes, and they are certainly not anthropoid. They have four arms and four legs, and what appear to be two heads, but these latter simply contain the sense organs, as the brain is in the body itself. In spite of their nightmarish appearance they are responsive creatures, quite ready to adopt those human manners, methods, and institutions which seem useful to them. This is especially true of the Royal Giants of the Trapezus, who have a settled existence in their caves. They derive their livelihood by a kind of agriculture, and their lichen terraces are extremely interesting. They are a gentle folk, and arouse themselves only against the rogues and outcasts who are of course much less amiable.

"I am sure we shall profit by our visit to Sirius Planet; more than this, we may be able to implant some glimmer of our musical heritage into a people curiously deficient in this regard. Who knows? Perhaps our visit will trigger a complete revolution in the life of the byzantaurs!"

Dame Isabel had a few more words to say: "You may well feel a certain awkwardness in performing before an alien people. All I can say is: do your best! We may of course make a few minor changes to conform with local sensibilities; you may feel a certain emptiness or lack of responsiveness in the audience—again all I say is: do your best!"

During the remarks of Dame Isabel and Bernard Bickel, Roger had sat to the back of the saloon, gloomily drinking champagne. Earlier, he had attempted to see Madoc Roswyn, but, as on all his previous attempts, she had refused to speak with him. Tiring of the babble and laughter, he left the saloon, paced the circumference of the ship, through each of the five globes and connecting tubes. Passing the bridge his spirits were not raised by the sight of Madoc Roswyn and Captain Gondar standing together by the forward port, looking ahead toward Sirius—or rather toward that image of Sirius converted by a dephasing mechanism from the compressed columns of light impinging upon the ship from ahead, and projected upon a screen. Captin Gondar had given over his office to Neil Henderson the Chief Technician, and moved Madoc Roswyn into the cabin thus vacated; she was wearing a pale blue coverall from the ship's stores.

Roger watched them for a few seconds. They were engaged in earnest conversation: a matter apparently concerning the route of the ship, for as Roger watched, Captain Gondar pointed off to the right of Sirius and Madoc Roswyn followed the line of his finger with her eyes.

Logan de Appling, the astrogator, appeared in the corridor: a slender young man with a craggy face, a poet's mop of curly brown hair, bright blue eyes. He looked at the bridge, shook his head in deprecation. "Do you know what I think?" he told Roger. "Captain Gondar is besotted. That's what I think." He turned swiftly and walked away.

Chapter Six

SIRIUS PLANET hung ahead, a dim gray world with heavy caps of overcast at the poles, a series of shallow equatorial seas, a pair of major land-masses, consisting of flat gray plains, mountain chains and smouldering volcanoes. The *Phoebus* swung in orbit twenty thousand miles above the planet; Captain Gondar located Sirius Settlement and radioed down a notification of arrival.

Acknowledgement and landing clearance presently returned; Gondar fed an appropriate landing program into the automatic pilot; the *Phoebus* veered off and down at a slant.

The dim gray ball grew larger, atmosphere soughed and hissed around the ship. Sirius Settlement was situated at the edge of Padway Plain, in the shadow of the towering Trapezus mountains, and here landed the *Phoebus*.

During the previous three days the atmosphere in the ship had been adjusted to the pressure and composition of the local air, and carefully metered drugs had been administered to passengers and crew to minimize the biological side-effects of the change, so now there was no delay. Directly upon landing the ports were opened, the off-ramp extended. Captain Gondar stepped forth with Dame Isabel, Bernard Bickel and other members of the company coming after. Overhead the sky was dark gray; Sirius shone with a cool white glare. A quarter-mile distant a line of white concrete buildings suggested a barracks rather than a trade and administrative outpost.

Commandant Dyrus Boltzen had come with one of his aides to meet the ship: a thin sandy-haired man with austere features and an air of dry skepticism. He now stepped briskly forward, with a curious stare for the chattering and ebullient company. "I'm Dyrus Boltzen, Commandant. Welcome to Sirius Settlement. It doesn't look like much at first sight—and believe me—it gets worse."

Captain Gandor laughed politely. "I'm Gondar, master of the ship. This is Dame Isabel Grayce, and Mr. Bernard Bickel, whom I belive you know."

"Yes, of course. Hello, Bickel. Nice to see you again."

"These other folk I won't introduce, but they're all famous musicians and opera singers."

Commandant Boltzen's straw-colored eyebrows shot up. "An opera company? What brings you here? There aren't any theaters on Sirius Planet."

Dame Isabel said, "We are equipped with our own theater, and with your permission propose to present a performance of *Fidelio.*"

Dyrus Boltzen scratched his head, looked over his shoulder at his side. He glanced at Bernard Bickel, who had turned away and was inspecting the landscape. He looked at Adolph Gondar who stared back impassively. He returned to Dame Isabel. "This is very nice—lovely, in fact—but there are only five Earth folk on the entire planet, and two of them are off on a prospect trip."

Dame Isabel said, "Naturally you will be welcome to the performance, but perhaps I had better explain. We like to think of ourselves as missionaries of music: we plan to perform before the intelligent alien races of the universe, who otherwise would have no experience of Earth music. The byzantaurs fall into this category."

Dyrus Boltzen rubbed his chin. "As I understand it, you propose to stage an opera for the byzantaurs?"

"Exactly. And not just an opera: *Fidelio!*"

Boltzen mused a moment or two. "One of my responsibilities is to prevent abuse or exploitation of the 'zants; I don't see how showing them an opera can hurt them."

"Assuredly not!"

"You don't plan to charge admission? Because if you

do, you're in for disappointment. The 'zants have no commercial sense whatever."

"If necessary, our performances will be staged free of charge, with absolutely no obligation."

Boltzen shrugged. "Go right ahead. I'll be interested to see what happens. You say you carry your own theater?"

"This is the case. Captain Gondar, will you be good enough to see to opening up the stage, and making ready the auditorium? And Andrei, perhaps you had better look to the sets."

"Certainly, madame. Of course." Captain Gondar and Andrei Szinc walked back onto the ship.

Dame Isabel looked around the landscape. "I had expected something rather more impressive. A city perhaps—some indication of aboriginal culture."

Boltzen laughed. "The byzantaurs are intelligent, no question about this. But they use their intelligence in line with their own pursuits, if you follow me."

"I'm afraid that I don't."

"Well, what I mean is this. They use their intelligence just as we use ours—to make life easier, more secure, more comfortable. They're clever with their rock-work and their lichen terraces—you can see them just up the hill— but down in their potholes they think thoughts which would puzzle us if we knew them."

"The byzantaurs are not articulate?" asked Dame Isabel. "Is there no exchange of ideas?"

"I wouldn't go quite that far. They're clever enough when they want to be—and a number of them speak our language with astounding proficiency. But all the time you wonder—you can't help but wonder—if it's nothing but clever mimicry."

"They have no written language? No pictorial skill?"

"The Royals who inhabit the Trapezus can read and write—at least some of them, and they have a mathematics of their own. Incidentally, it's a mathematics which none of our mathematicians can understand. But I'm only glancing around the subject of the 'zants. To know a folk like this, even superficially, you have to live with them for years."

"But what of music?" persisted Dame Isabel. "Do they have any ear for music, do they compose, is there a native musical idiom?"

"I suspect not," said Dyrus Boltzen with careful courtesy. "But of course I can't be entirely sure. I have held this station down for six years, but I still keep running into things which surprise me."

Dame Isabel nodded brusquely. She did not find Dyrus Boltzen's manner ingratiating, though he had given her no specific cause for resentment. She now ceremoniously introduced the members of the company, watching Dyrus Boltzen sidelong as she spoke the famous names, but they seemed to mean nothing. "As I suspected," she told herself. "The man is a musical illiterate.

Dyrus Boltzen took the group on a tour of the settlement, which consisted of little more than four concrete buildings surrounding a bleak compound. Two of the buildings were warehouses for trade-goods: one for imports, the other for articles to be exported—bowls, salvers, vases, goblets and dinner services polished from native stone: translucent obsidian, turquoise, jade, carnelian, a dense blue dumortierite, black basalt. There were jewels and crystals, chandeliers with pendants of diamonds, emeralds and sapphires, tourmaline windchimes. In the compound the group saw its first byzantaurs, a team of four equipped with brooms and water-sprays, sweeping the concrete expanse with great care and concentration. They were even more grotesque than their photographs had indicated: an impression furthered by the motion of their four arms and four legs, the working of the oddly placed features in the two heads, the texture of the skin, as rough and grey as rock.

Dame Isabel spoke to Dyrus Boltzen: "The creatures seem cooperative, even mild."

Boltzen laughed. "Those four are what, for lack of a better word, we call elders. Every day, for some reason quite beyond my comprehension, they sweep the compound. Notice the shawl around the neck? That's a fabric woven of rock fiber. The colors are significant by the way, almost like the old Scottish tartans. The brown and blue and black are characteristic of the Royal Giants, and the length of the fringe is a measure of prestige or rank." He summoned one of the byzantaurs; it approached on thick stiff legs which clicked against the concrete. "Friend 'zant," said Boltzen, "here are people from the sky. They come in big ship. They like to show all friend 'zants many pretty things. They like friend 'zants to come to ship. Okay?"

From somewhere deep inside the thorax came a rumbling voice. "Maybe okay. Friend 'zants scared."

Dame Isabel stepped forward. "You need fear nothing. We are a legitimate grand opera company, we will perform a program we are sure you will enjoy."

"Maybe okay, we go to look for yellow no-good 'zants. Maybe not scared."

Boltzen explained. "He's not literally afraid, it's only that they dislike to come up from their tunnels any more than necessary; they feel that it's demeaning."

"Interesting! But why should this be?"

"It's a matter of social standing. They eject their criminals and nonconformists upon the plain where they become either rogues or bands of what might be termed psychotics. So you see the plain represents an undesirable environment to the 'zants."

"I understand fully," said Dame Isabel. "Well, the performance will take place inside the ship, and they will be spared the indignity of watching from the plain."

Boltzen turned to the elder. "You hear sky-talk? He show pretty things, pretty noise, not on plain, but inside ship. You and friend 'zants run over plain and go inside ship to look. Okay?"

"Okay. I go down, talk to friend 'zants."

Bernard Bickel remained with Commandant Boltzen to talk over old times, while the rest of the group returned to the *Phoebus*. A transformation already had taken place. Under the guidance of Captain Gondar a tall pole had

been erected in the center of the pentagonal space enclosed by the tubes and globes. Guy-wires were now
strung, and over all were drawn sheets of a metalloid fabric, creating a tent. The stage had been opened, the orchestra pit extended, and when Dame Isabel came to make
an inspection she found Madoc Roswyn carefully arranging the collapsible benches around the area. "Hmmf!" said
Dame Isabel to herself. "Trying to make herself useful, so
that I won't put her ashore." She chuckled grimly, and
looked about for Roger, but he was nowhere in sight.

Bernard Bickel presently strolled up. "I've had an interesting chat with Commandant Boltzen, and I think I was
able to put across our point of view. He still is a trifle dubious, but he agrees that no harm can be done and quite
possibly some good."

Dame Isabel snorted. "Indeed I should think so!"

"He also asks that you, I and Captain Gondar join him
for dinner, when perhaps he'll be able to give us more information regarding the byzantaurs."

"That is exceedingly gracious of him," said Dame Isabel, "I shall be glad to go."

"I assumed as much and accepted the invitation for all
of us."

Three hours later Sirius hung close above the horizon,
its lower edge touching a bank of soft white mist at the far
edge of the plain. The company had gathered outside to
watch the coming of twilight and a very impressive sight it
was, as Sirius drifted into the clouds, which immediately
became suffused with nacreous pinks and greens.

Dame Isabel, Captain Gondar and Bernard Bickel set
off for their dinner engagement. Roger, who wandered
morosely off across the plain, now returned to the ship
where he became an unintentional eaves-dropper. He had
stopped to watch the Sirius-set beside the off-ramp, unaware that Madoc Roswyn and Logan de Appling were sitting on the bottom step, with a canvas panel hiding Roger
from their view.

Roger recognized Madoc Roswyn's slightly husky voice

and stood transfixed. "Logan, please don't speak like that—you're really quite wrong."

"No, I'm not wrong!" De Appling's voice quivered with the intensity of his emotion. "You don't know him as I do!"

Captain Gondar has been more than kind to me; he's treated me with complete consideration, and never tried to force himself upon me, like that unmentionable Roger Wool."

Roger's ears burned and his skin felt crisp and brittle as if a chill wind were playing across his face.

"He's just softening you up," argued de Appling. "He's a hard man, my darling—"

"Please don't call me that, Logan."

"—he's self-centered and unprincipled. I know! I've seen him in action."

"No, Logan, don't say things like that. He's helping me stay aboard the ship, he's promised Dame Isabel won't put me off. What more could he do for me?"

There was a short silence as de Appling mulled over what she had said. Roger did the same.

Logan de Appling spoke in a neutral voice: "Why is it so important that you make the trip?"

"Oh—I don't know." And Roger could visualize the charming little twist of shoulder, the tilt of head and curve of mouth. "I just want to, I suppose. Would you like me to get off?"

"You know better than that. But tell me, tell me, please, that you won't—"

"Won't what, Logan?" asked Madoc Roswyn sweetly.

"Won't let Adolph Gondar take advantage of you!" de Appling exclaimed fiercely. "The thought gives me the cold shudders. I think I'd kill him, or myself, or do something terrible . . . Wreck the whole ghastly ship . . ."

"Now, Logan, don't be impulsive. Let's just watch the lovely Sirius-set. Isn't it magnificent? And so strange and eerie! I'd never imagined that one sunset could be so different from another!"

Roger took a deep breath, walked quietly away, around the entire circumference of the ship.

* * * * * *

Dyrus Boltzen provided an unexpectedly good dinner, due, he admitted, to the fact that the supply ship had departed Sirius Settlement only about three weeks previously. "We're close to Earth here—relatively of course—yet this is a lonely planet. Very few casuals like yourself put in. None of them, naturally, with an ambitious program like yours."

"Do you think that we can make ourselves comprehensible to the byzantaurs?" asked Dame Isabel. "They seem completely non-human in their attitudes."

"In certain ways, yes, in others, no. Sometimes I wonder at how closely our judgments mesh. Other times I'm just as astonished that we could view the same simple act from such different angles. I'll say this much: if you want to present a program that the byzantaurs can relate to their own existence, you're going to have to take them on their own terms."

"Naturally," said Bernard Bickel. "We are prepared to do so. Can you offer us suggestions?"

Boltzen poured wine all around. "I believe I can. Let me see. An obvious matter is color, to which they are highly sensitive. Yellow is the color of rogues and outcasts, so the unsympathetic characters should wear yellow, the hero and heroine blue or black, and those in supporting roles gray and green. There is the matter of sex: love, romance, whatever you want to call it. The 'zants have peculiar reproductive habits; in fact there are three sex processes, and each of the 'zants is capable of performing two of them, so you can see that an untold number of misunderstandings might ensue unless a certain allowance were made for this fact. They do not demonstrate affection by hugging or kissing: their sex play is a matter of spraying the intended mate with a viscous liquid. I doubt if you wish to carry similitude to quite this extent."

"Probably not," agreed Bernard Bickel.

"Well, let's think further . . . as I recall *Fidelio*—are not certain scenes played in a dungeon?"

"Quite correct," said Dame Isabel. "Almost the whole of Act Two."

"You must remember that a dungeon is a cherished home to the 'zants. The deranged, the troublemakers are expelled to the plain, where they roam in bands: incidentally, warn your company not to wander off by themselves. The rogues are not automatically savage, but are highly unpredictable, especially when they carry their flints."

"Well, well, well," said Dame Isabel slowly. "I suppose we can make scene changes easily enough: perhaps play Act One in the dungeon and the first scene of Act Two in the open."

"If you're trying to get your point across, I suggest something on this order."

"Oh indeed we are," declared Dame Isabel. "Why come all this way merely to confuse our audience?"

"Why indeed?" echoed Bernard Bickel.

"Then there's also costuming. Do you know what the 'zants call us in their own language? Sky-lice. Exactly. Their feelings toward us are, as closely as I can gather, amiable contempt. We are a race to be exploited, a set of eccentrics who will trade intricate metal devices for fragments of polished rock!"

Dame Isabel looked rather helplessly toward Bernard Bickel, who fingered his mustache. "I hope," she said uncertainly, "that the performance will do something to alter their view."

"Again—and I don't know if you care to go this far—but from the standpoint of your audience the production would make more sense if they could identify themselves and their own lives with the actors and the course of action."

"We can't rewrite the opera," complained Dame Isabel. "We wouldn't be presenting *Fidelio,* which of course is our intent."

"I appreciate this; I am making no recommendations, only supplying information on which you may or may not choose to act. For instance, if you costumed your 'sky-lice' players to resemble byzantaurs, you'd command a much higher degree of attention."

"This is all very well," protested Dame Isabel, "but where in the world would we scrape up such complicated costumes? Impossible!"

"I could help to some extent," said Dyrus Boltzen. He poured more wine and ruminated, while Dame Isabel and Bernard Bickel watched him attentively. "I have in the warehouse," he said at last, "a number of tanned byzantaur pelts which are destined for the British Museum. They would serve quite well as costumes, or so I would think. If you like I'll have them brought to your ship. All I ask is that you take good care of them."

"That's very kind of you," said Dame Isabel. "Mr. Bickel, what is your opinion?"

Bernard Bickel blinked. "Well—I certainly agree that if our object is to interest the non-Earthly folk of the cosmos in music—specifically, our Earthly music—then we're going to have to make very earnest and whole-hearted efforts."

Dame Isabel nodded decisively. "Yes. That certainly is what we must do."

"I'll send the skins over to your ship," said Dyrus Boltzen.

"One more matter," Dame Isabel put forward. "I have set curtain-time for tomorrow at three hours after noon, whatever this is called by your local time."

"Three o'clock," said Dyrus Boltzen. "Our day is twenty hours and twelve minutes long, so noon and midnight both come at six minutes after ten. Three o'clock should do very nicely."

"I trust that you will do your best to see that the byzantaurs come to the performance?"

"I will do my best, indeed I will. And I'll get the 'zant skins over to your ship first thing in the morning." And Dyrus Boltzen raised his glass. "To a successful performance!"

* * * * * * *

The night was dark. From over the plain and down from the mountain came strange noises: soft hoots, occasionally a far jarring screech, once or twice a mournful fluting. Neither Bernard Bickel nor Captain Gondar could positively identify the source of the sounds, and agreed in ascribing them to lower life-forms of the planet.

No one wandered far from the ship, though there was an undeniable thrill in moving fifty or a hundred feet away from the off-ramp and standing in the night of Sirius Planet, looking up at the distorted constellations, and listening to the eery sounds.

Shortly after four o'clock the sky lightened and at five Sirius, a blazing white pellet, rose above the Trapezus Mountains. An hour or two later Commandant Boltzen, true to his word, delivered a jeep-load of byzantaur skins.

Hermilda Warn, who took the role of Leonore in *Fidelio,* emitted a gasp of dismay. She turned to Dame Isabel. "You surely do not expect us to wear those things?"

"Yes, of course," said Dame Isabel calmly. "It is a concession to the social sensibilities of our audience."

Herman Scantling, who sang Pizarro, threw his hands in the air. "Perhaps you will inform me how I can express myself with four arms? And which of the two heads I should use to cover my own? And how, conceivably how, can I achieve a projection behind these wads and folds?"

"The skins smell quite badly," said Otto von Scheerup, who sang the part of Florestan. "I think the idea is absolutely ridiculous."

Dame Isabel's mouth became a thin white line. "There will be no argument. There are the costumes for this afternoon's performance, and I will brook no insubordination. Your contracts are quite specific on this point. You are not required to risk your health; but a certain amount of discomfort must be expected and tolerated cheerfully. I will not put up with temperamental outbursts, and that is all there is to be said on the subject." She turned to Roger, who stood nearby. "Here, Roger, is an opportunity to make yourself useful. Take these pelts to Mr. Szinc in the dressing rooms and help him fit them to those persons taking part in today's performance."

Roger, grimacing fastidiously, approached the pelts. Hermilda Warn heaved an outraged sigh. "I have never known such outrageous circumstances!"

Dame Isabel ignored her and walked over to confer with Dyrus Boltzen.

Herman Scantling asked, "Has there ever been anything so fantastic?"

Otto von Scheerup shook his head in a surly fashion. "Wait till we report this to the Guild! All I can say is, just wait! Fur will fly!"

"But—in the meantime?" asked Ramona Thoxted, who sang Marcellina. "Must we wear the odious things?"

Herman Scantling gave a sour grunt. "She'd put us off on this God-forsaken ball of rocks, without salary, without tickets home, without anything."

"We could sue," asserted Julia Biancolelli, somewhat feebly.

Neither Herman Scantling, Hermilda Warn, nor Otto von Scheerup made reply, and Romona Thoxted said, "I suppose that on a tour of this sort we must be ready for almost anything."

The morning passed, and at six minutes after ten became afternoon. At one-thirty Dyrus Boltzen and his aide flew down in a platform flyer. Dyrus Boltzen wore whipcord breeches, heavy boots, a hooded jacket. At his belt hung a weapon. He went to where Dame Isabel sat making last minute alterations in the libretto: "Sorry, but I'll have to miss the performance. We've got to look to some unpleasant business. A band of very uncertain rogues has been seen heading this way, and we have to turn them aside before they make trouble on the terraces."

"That's a shame!" declared Dame Isabel. "After you've done so much to help! You did arrange that the local folk should come to the performance?"

"Oh yes. They know all about it, and at three o'clock they'll be here. With luck I'll be back to catch the last act!" He returned to the flyer, which slid off to the north.

"A shame he must miss the opera, but I suppose there's no help for it," said Dame Isabel. "Now then, everyone. The word 'dungeon' is not to be used. We substitute the word 'desert!' "

"What difference does it make?" inquired Herman Scantling. "We sing in German which the local beasts can't understand in the first place."

Dame Isabel spoke with the mildness that warned the more knowing of her associates. "Our aim, Mr. Scantling, is for faithfulness, for a basic intensity. If the scene represents a desert, as it now does, then a falsity is committed in referring to this desert as a dungeon, even in German. Do I make myself clear?"

"The meter is changed," growled Otto von Scheerup. " 'Die Wuste,' 'der Burgverliesz.' "

"You must do your best."

Three o'clock approached. The musicians assembled in the orchestra pit, Sir Henry Rixon appeared, glanced briefly through the score. Back-stage, amid objurgations, muttered obscenities, exclamations of distress, the byzantaur pelts were donned and costumes fitted as well as possible.

At five minutes to three Dame Isabel went to look across the plain. "Our audience certainly should be on its way," she told Bernard Bickel. "I do hope there hasn't been some misunderstanding as to time."

"Damned nuisance that Boltzen was called away," said Bickel. "Maybe the 'zants are waiting for someone to bring them over, or something of the sort. They're a bit dubious of the open ground, if you recall what Boltzen told us."

"Quite true. Perhaps, Bernard, you had best stroll over to the caves and see what may be the matter."

Bickel frowned, sucked at his mustache, but was able to evolve no counter-proposal. He set off toward the station, and Dame Isabel went back-stage to make sure that all was proceeding properly. She shook her head in dismay. Where was the dignity, the easy elegance she had envisioned? Certainly not here among these angry tenors, sopranos and basses. Some wore caps on one of the heads, others had thrust two of the four arms through the sleeves of their capes, with the others hanging over their shoulders. Dame Isabel turned on her heel and departed.

At quarter after three Roger came to tell her that Bernard Bickel had returned with the byzantaurs.

"Excellent!" said Dame Isabel. "You will kindly assist with the seating, Roger. Remember, the longer the fringe of that little shawl, the more exalted the personage."

Roger nodded, hurried out to make himself useful. Bernard Bickel came in to report to Dame Isabel. "They were on their way, just coming in from some kind of walkabout, probably why they were late. I dragooned them along and here they are."

Dame Isabel looked through the peep-hole and saw that the auditorium indeed was full of byzantaurs. In large numbers they seemed even more strange and inhuman than before—even somewhat alarming. Dame Isabel hesitated, then stepped out before the curtain to make a welcoming address.

"Ladies and gentlemen, I welcome you to our little performance. You are about to see the opera *Fidelio*, by Ludwig von Beethoven, one of our most accomplished composers. We bring you this program in the hope that some of you may wish to learn more about the great music of Earth. And now, since I am not sure just how much of what I say is comprehensible to you, I now will retire and let the music speak for itself. We bring you: *Fidelio!*"

Sir Henry Rixon snapped down his baton: music filled the auditorium.

Dame Isabel went down the off-ramp, stood by the entrance to the auditorium listening to the overture. How wonderful it sounded here on Sirius Planet! How moving to have this glorious essence, this seventh distillation of Earthly civilization permeating the Sirius air, entering into the soul of these pathetically ugly and unprivileged people! Would the experience ennoble them, lift them beyond their rock-grubbing existences, convey even so much as a tenth of the beauty and exaltation inherent in the music? A pity, thought Dame Isabel; she would never be sure.

The curtain rose on the first act; Marcellina and Jacquino, in byzantaur pelts, sang of love and longing; and playing before the audience of byzantaurs, the costumes were not quite so insanely ludicrous as they had seemed before. But here came Dyrus Boltzen and his aide. Dame Isabel waved her hand; Dyrus Boltzen waved a weary hand in return. Dame Isabel stepped forth to meet him.

"Dreadfully sorry about everything," he said heavily. "I didn't have time to tell you, but I knew they wouldn't come today. They'd be too cautious."

Dame Isabel raised her eyebrows questioningly. "Who wouldn't come? The byzantaurs? They're here. We have a full house!"

Dyrus Boltzen stared at her in surprise. "They're here? I can't believe it. They'd never leave their caves with the rogues coming over the mountains."

Dame Isabel smilingly disagreed. "But they did. They're here and enjoying the music immensely."

Dyrus Boltzen went to the entrance, peered within. He backed slowly out. He turned to face Dame Isabel, his face twitching through a series of ashen expressions. "Your audience," he said in a queer voice, "consists of the rogues—the psychotic outcasts of whom the Royal Giants are terrified."

"What? Are you sure?"

"Yes. They're wearing their yellow; can't you see? And they're carrying flints, which means they're in an ugly mood!"

Dame Isabel wrung her hands. "What shall I do? Stop the show?"

"I don't know," said Boltzen. "The slightest stimulus will set them off."

"But what *can* we do?" whispered Dame Isabel.

"Don't irritate them in any way. Make no sudden noises. Also you'd better change your scoring back to the original; any reference to their condition sends them blind with rage."

Dame Isabel ran back-stage. "Change everything!" she

cried. "Back to the original version; we've got a different audience!"

Otto von Scheerup looked at her unbelievingly. "A different audience? What do you mean?"

"These are savages, and worse! At the slightest pretext they'll cause a serious disturbance!"

Otto von Scheerup glanced uncertainly out toward the stage. Hermilda Warn sang Fidelio's pity for Marcellina's misguided love. She reached for the kerchief with which it was her habit to underscore her gestures; Dame Isabel ran out on the stage, snatched it from her hands. "It's yellow," she hissed at the startled diva, and ran back off the stage.

Through the peep-hole she watched the audience. They were shifting restlessly in their seats, heads moving and twisting in a rather frightening fashion. She asked, "Where is Mr. Bickel?"

Andrei Szinc pointed. "Down in the audience, explaining the opera to that large creature with the stone club."

"What a terrible situation!" cried Dame Isabel. She ran through the ship to Globe A and the bridge, where she found Captain Gondar kissing Madoc Roswyn.

"Captain Gondar!" called Dame Isabel in a voice like a horn. "If you will put aside your private affairs, there is a serious emergency with which we must deal." As succinctly as possible she described the circumstances.

Captain Gondar gave a terse nod, spoke a few words into the intercom, alerting the crew. Then, followed by Dame Isabel, he strode through the connecting tubes to the stage.

Dame Isabel went back to the peep-hole. The audience was decidedly restive. Certain of the rogues, on their four feet, stood swaying, waving their arms, tapping their heads together. On the stage, the singers had become mesmerized by the motion, and were faltering. Sir Henry Rixon gave an energetic beat to the orchestra, but from the audience came a new distraction.

Bernard Bickel, in the audience, had been sitting beside that rogue whom he had identified as the chief elder, making such comments as the limited comprehension of the byzantaur seemed to warrant. Apparently he had noticed neither the yellow shawl nor the flint-studded club, or perhaps mistook the latter for an article of strictly ceremonial function. He never was able to recall the precise remark which irritated the byzantaur; in any event the creature raised his club with the clear intent of halting Bernard Bickel's commentary. But he underestimated the resource of the musicologist, who had faced such emergencies before. Bickel struck the elder on the right head with his fist, fended aside the blow of the club and leapt into the orchestra pit, where he fell among the percussion instruments. The sudden discordant clash of cymbals seemed to excite the byzantaurs: they rumbled, groaned, and waving their flints converged upon Bernard Bickel and the orchestra at large.

All who were able scrambled for the stage, those nearest the auditorium fending off the rogues with their instruments. Captain Gondar leapt forth, shouting orders, while members of the crew rigged fire-hoses.

On the stage one of the singers from sheer hysteria jumped from his pelt and threw it at the audience, which caused instant alarm among the unstable rogues. Others did likewise, hooting and jeering, and the byzantaurs drew back. Now water gushed from the high pressure hoses and the byzantaurs were spewed from the theater, out upon the plain, where they picked themselves up and set off to the north at an awkward lope.

A half-hour later some semblance of order had been restored. Dame Isabel, Bernard Bickel, Captain Gondar, Sir Henry Rixon, Andrei Szinc, and a number of musicians and singers had gathered in the main saloon. Commandant Boltzen tried to provide a dispassionate analysis of the incident, but his voice was submerged in the babble.

Finally, Dyrus Boltzen was able to make himself heard. "Tomorrow will be different! I'll have the Royal Giants here for absolute certain—no flints either!"

There was a sudden silence in the room. Andrei Szinc went to speak to Sir Henry Rixon, who nodded and took Dame Isabel aside. Her mouth compressed; she drew a deep breath as if to make a forceful statement; then she hesitated, and finally gave a short nod. To Dyrus Boltzen she said, "I fear there will be no other performance at Sirius Settlement. Certain of the musicians are indisposed, and others are—well, also indisposed. We will be departing as soon as the *Phoebus* can be made ready for space."

Chapter Seven

IN THE excitement attendant upon the company's first performance, Dame Isabel failed to remember her intent to put Madoc Roswyn ashore at Sirius Settlement, and Madoc Roswyn stayed discreetly out of sight.

When Dame Isabel did remember, she clicked her tongue in annoyance. Considering Captain Gondar's obvious infatuation she clicked her tongue again, and debated whether or not to make an issue of the situation. Rather reluctantly she decided it was none of her affair, and when she conferred with Captain Gondar regarding the next port of call, Madoc Roswyn was not mentioned. "According to our itinerary," said Dame Isabel in her most formal voice, "we will next visit the second planet of Phi Orionis. Mr. Bickel tells me that the authochthones are definitely humanoid; is that not right, Bernard?"

Bickel, who had just entered the cabin, replied in the affirmative. "I have not visited the world myself, but I understand that the inhabitants of Zade are not only humanoid in appearance, but also display cultural traits analogous to our own, including art forms based on the modulation of sound. Which is to say: music."

"Zade then it is," said Dame Isabel. "I presume, Captain, that our route will not take us too far afield from Rlaru?"

"No," said Gondar grudgingly. "No difficulty there: Phi Orion is the general direction. But I have a suggestion."

Dame Isabel cocked her head in polite inquiry. "Yes?"

"I recall mention of a planet in Hydra inhabited by a very musical people. It's a world which has hardly been visited by man, and I understand that it's extremely advanced artistically. Just the place for you to take your troupe, or so it seems to me."

Dame Isabel gave him a sharp glance. Captain Gondar's tone had rung almost inperceptibly false. "Our present itinerary, according to you, takes us toward Rlaru. Is this not correct?"

"Yes indeed. Absolutely correct."

Bickel said. "Come to think of it, Gondar, don't you think it's time you let us in on the location of Rlaru? After all, we're neither thugs nor hijackers, and we obviously don't plan to victimize you in any way."

Gondar's long sallow face creased in a slight smile. "Better that I keep my own counsel—for a very good reason."

"But suppose something happened to you!" exclaimed Bernard Bickel. "Then we'd be unable to find Rlaru, which is our principal goal!"

Captain Gondar shook his head stubbornly.

"I fail to understand your reluctance to trust us," said Dame Isabel. "You certain can't believe that we would attempt to bamboozle you?"

"Of course not, and I'm sorry if I give that impression."

"Why then are you so unnaturally cautious?"

Captain Gondar reflected a moment. "I'll be quite frank," he said. "You put matters on the basis of trust, but your demands for information make it clear that you do not trust me. This arouses in me a counter-distrust. You control a great deal of money which is rightfully mine, and this is leverage you exert upon me. I have information you want and this is my leverage upon you. You are asking me to give up my leverage, to put myself in your power, without making a corresponding concession."

Dame Isabel gave a puzzled little shake of her head. "What you say might be sensible on Earth—but out here, en route to Rlaru, what do you gain? Both Mr. Bickel and I are persons of honor; I can't imagine us—for the sake of argument—marooning you, or—to be really melodramatic—causing your death."

"Stranger things have happened," said Captain Gondar with his most saturnine smile.

Dame Isabel sniffed. "You are quite impossible, Captain Gondar."

"If we had criminal designs upon you," Bernard Bickel argued, "we could achieve them just as easily *after* we left Rlaru, *after* you took us there, as now. In fact, if we were the sort you believe us to be, we would make sure that you had given us accurate directions *before* putting you out of the way."

Captain Gondar shook his head. "Let's drop the subject. When the time comes, I will take you to Rlaru. When the time comes, I hope that you in your turn will give me my money."

"I suppose we have no choice in the matter," said Dame Isabel stiffly.

"Now as to the matter of the planet I mentioned—I believe a visit to this planet would be highly rewarding."

"That well may be. Reverting once more to Rlaru, in what configurational sector does it lie?"

"In Cetus," said Captain Gondar with poor grace.

"Well then—a visit to this planet in Hydra would take us almost directly away from Rlaru. We would be forced to make a tedious detour. Am I not correct?"

Captain Gondar seemed almost obsequious. "A slight detour perhaps—but a very rewarding one. Indeed, I think it would be a great mistake to avoid the planet; the folk are quite humanoid—almost human, I would say—"

Bernard Bickel frowned. "In Hydra? I don't recall any such planet in Hydra."

Dame Isabel asked, "What is the source of your information?"

"An old explorer described it to me," said Gondar, again with the faintly brassy heartiness which previously had aroused Dame Isabel's suspicion. "Ever since, I have wanted to visit this planet."

"You must do so on some other occasion," said Dame Isabel decisively. "Our current itinerary is already established; we cannot jerk here and there about the galaxy to gratify a single person's whim. I am sorry, Captain Gondar."

Gondar turned on his heel, started for the door. Dame Isabel said to his back: "Kindly notify the astrogator that our immediate destination is Zade, the second planet of Phi Orionis."

When the door had slid shut behind Gondar, Bernard Bickel turned to Dame Isabel, his eyebrows arched, his blue eyes round in puzzlement. "Odd! Why in the name of all the lesser demons is Gondar so anxious to visit this particular world?"

Dame Isabel had already dismissed the matter from her mind. "It makes small difference, since we will not be doing so."

* * * * * * *

While Dame Isabel and Bernard Bickel conferred with Captain Gondar, Roger Wool, wandering aimlessly about the ship, passed across the stage in Globe C. The musicians and singers had completed their daily rehearsals, but the stage still retained a memory of their presence: an exhalation of perfume, camphor, rosin, and valve-oil. A single dim light illuminated the stage, and sitting quietly on one of the stage-property chairs was Madoc Roswyn.

She saw Roger without change of expression. Roger slowly approached. He said, "I wish you'd tell me why you acted the way you did—told those terrible stories about me . . . As if I'd ever force you to do anything against your will . . ."

She made a flippant gesture. "It seemed a good thing at the time. You must recognize, Roger, that I am fickle and perverse: not at all the girl you thought I was."

"I can't escape the feeling that you were using me, but to what end I can't imagine . . . Once I thought you were fond of me. If you were, if you still are—for heaven's sake tell me, and we'll clear up this terrible misunderstanding."

"There's no misunderstanding, Roger." Madoc Roswyn's voice was gentle, but absolutely toneless.

Roger looked at her a moment, then shook his head.

"How can anyone so beautiful, so sensitive, so clever, be so faithless? I can't understand!"

"It's not necessary that you understand, Roger. Now run off and find your aunt. She has an errand for you."

Roger turned on his heel, departed the stage. Madoc Roswyn watched him go with no expression other than a peculiar pinched look which might have meant one of a dozen things.

* * * * * * *

Roger, continuing moodily around the ship, encountered his aunt in the corridor outside the saloon, where she had been listening to the complaints of Ada Francini, regarding certain odd sounds.

Dame Isabel's eye fell on Roger, and indeed there was an errand for him to perform.

"Roger, have you noticed a grating thumping sound in Globe D? It occurs at irregular intervals and seems to come from nowhere in particular."

"I hadn't noticed," said Roger dully.

"Miss Francini tells me that this sound is seriously disturbing the rest of the company. She said something about it to Captain Gondar, but he took very little interest."

"Somebody snoring?" asked Roger.

"I thought of that too, but Miss Francini says the sound is quite unlike a snore."

Again Roger stated that he had not noticed this particular sound.

"Well, I want you to find what causes it, and if the source is mechanical, call it to the attention of the Chief Technician."

Roger agreed to do his best, and slouched off toward Globe D. He knocked at the cubicle which Ephraim Zerner shared with Otto von Scheerup and inquired for particulars regarding the offensive noises.

Both Zerner and von Scheerup supplied information, though they were not in precise agreement. Ephraim Zerner mentioned a reedy whistling sound which occasionally accompanied the throbbing and rasping, while von

Scheerup emphasized a "bumping and booming, which together with the rattling and squealing creates a most fearful racket." The sound occurred unpredictably, at intervals of a day or two, persisting sometimes for two hours or even longer.

Roger made other inquiries among the company. Some were more troubled than others; everyone had his own definition as to the essential quality of the sound, though all agreed as to its painful nature.

Roger walked here and there around Globe D, but the disagreeable sound did not manifest itself. He spoke once more to Ada Francini and asked that she notify him the instant the noise started, whereupon he would make a more careful investigation.

Six hours later the occasion offered itself. Ada Francini sought out Roger, who, as good as his word, returned with her to Globe D. Ada Francini took him to her cabin, raised up her finger. "Listen!"

Roger listened. Distinctly he heard the sound in question. He was forced to admit that no one had described it incorrectly, for it comprised a whole variety of rasping, rattling, booming, bumping, squealing, whining and throbbing noises. The sound seemed to come from the wall, from the air, from everywhere, from nowhere.

He stepped into the corridor and the sound became fainter. Carefully he maneuvered through the cabin and finally ascertained that the basic sound of the sound was the air-conditioning duct. Putting his ear to the mesh, he listened for several minutes. Then he rose to his feet, dusted off his knees. "I have a notion as to what is causing the noise," he told Ada Francini, "but first I'd better check more extensively."

An hour later Dame Isabel found Roger sitting in the saloon playing solitaire. "Well, Roger?" she demanded. "What have you been doing? Miss Francini tells me that the rattling sound is worse than ever and furthermore she says that you know what causes it."

"Yes, I did manage to track it down," said Roger. "It

comes from the crew's mess-hall in Globe E and travels by
the air-duct into Globe D."

"Indeed! And what goes on in the crew's mess-hall to
occasion such a clatter?"

"Well—it seems that certain members of the crew have
formed a washboard band."

"A *what?*"

"A *what?*" inquired Bernard Bickel who had entered
the saloon.

Roger explained as well as he could the instrumentation
and rationale of the Tough Luck Jug Bank, as the group
was known in the mess-hall. When in full voice, there
might be heard banjo, harmonica, washboard, kazoo, tub-
bass, jug, and occasionally a nose-flute.

Dame Isabel sat with an expression of utter disbelief.
"But why in the world should the crew want to create this
pandemonium? A group of children in high spirits will
beat on pots and pans—"

"They play various tunes," said Roger. "It's actually
rather lively."

"What nonsense," said Dame Isabel. "Bernard, have
you ever heard the like?"

Bernard Bickel shook his head in disparagement.
"Whatever they call the racket, we can't have it disturbing
everybody aboard."

"Please see to it, Bernard. My word, what will they
think of next?"

* * * * * * *

Space, that dark emptiness which when related to a system of stars almost palpable as an ocean separa-
ting a group of islands, passed astern—if emptiness can be
said to do anything whatsoever. And yet, something
passed astern, for Sirius receded and Phi Orionis approached, and in order to achieve this effect, a significant
process evidently was underway. Roger, wandering
through the saloon, picked up a book and read a trifle of
speculation from the pen of the eminent cosmologist Den-
nis Kertesz: "Infinity is a fascinating idea with which all of

us have struggled. Especially the infinity of extension, which cannot be evaded by proposing a universe of finite circumference. Less carefully considered is an infinity in the other direction: the infinity of smallness, and it extends as far and is as bemusing as that other infinity.

"What happens to matter at the lower reaches? Matter exhibits a constantly finer texture, until it no longer can be dealt with experimentally, or even mathematically. Eventually, or so it would seem, all matter, all energy, all everything, even space itself, must be expressed by some single antithesis: a basic yes or no; back or forth; in or out; clock-wise or counter-clockwise; fourth-dimensional coiling in, or fourth-dimensional coiling out. Even at this level, the infinite recession into smallness continues. No matter how small is anything it serves only as a gauge by which to define extremes (if only formal extremes) a hundred times smaller . . ."

Roger, already suffering melancholy, found the cosmic immensities appalling, and laid aside the book.

Bernard Bickel pointed out to him that space as observed from the *Phoebus* was essentially no different from space as observed from the terrace at Ballew on a clear night. Roger agreed in principle, but became only slightly less depressed in consequence.

Ahead Phi Orionis grew bright, and the day came when the second planet Zade could be seen, and presently the *Phoebus* went into landing orbit.

The Resident Commissioner at Earth-town radioed up a landing clearance; down to Zade settled the *Phoebus*.

Chapter Eight

LIKE MOST inhabited planets of the galaxy, Zade was a highly diversified world physiographically. There was a single continent which sprawled around two-thirds of the globe, with dozens of arms, inlets, peninsulas, extensions, fjords, capes and bays. Earth-town, a complex of warehouse, dormitories and administrative buildings, was situated on the banks of a river a few miles inland from the South Ocean. The Resident Commissioner, Edgar Cam, a tall thoughtful man with a big nose, big chin, big hands and feet, and a manner of cautious deliberation, attempted to discourage Dame Isabel from her purpose.

Sitting in Dame Isabel's cabin he explained his pessimism. "Theoretically I have no argument with your goals. The natives of Zade are by and large neither hostile, nor uncooperative: they are simply unpredictable. There are at least sixteen variations of the intelligent species, much more disparate than the races of man, and with their difference of color and anatomy go cultural differences. I couldn't even begin to generalize on them."

"They are a humanoid people?"

"Yes indeed. No question about that. From a distance of a hundred yards you can hardly distinguish one from a man."

"And I understand they are, in a sense, artists? That is to say, they understand the creative process, the sublimation of fact to symbol and the use of symbol to suggest emotion?"

"Absolutely, though here again there is great diversity as to ways and means. One of the peculiar facets of life on

72

Zade is the lack of cultural interchange. Each tribe seems to live sufficient to itself, and except for an occasional slave-raid, takes very little notice of its neighbors."

Dame Isabel frowned. "Do I understand you to say that in performing before audiences on Zade we would be in danger of physical harm or personal molestation?"

"Quite possibly, if you were rash enough to venture into the Brownback Mountains, or attempt to play before the Stagag-Ogog Clawbills. But these are isolated cases, and in general the folk of Zade are no more and no less to be feared than the people of Earth—if you assiduously heed their special conventions and habits—and herein lies the unpredictability of Zade."

"I think you can trust us on that score," said Bernard Bickel. "We are not exactly greenhorns, and naturally we will make every conceivable allowance for native peculiarities."

"Nevertheless," said Dame Isabel, "I would be happy if you would arrange a suitable itinerary for us, so that we could play before those tribes which would profit the most."

"I can suggest an itinerary," said Cam rather pedantically; "I cannot arrange one. Our situation here by no means affords us automatic respect. In fact, quite the contrary: certain of the tribes are sure Earth is a place of desolation and misery; why else would we go to such exertion to come to other worlds? In any event I have no authority beyond the precincts of the enclave, and if you ran afoul somewhere I'd be powerless to help you. By and large, there is no particular risk, but I stress the fact that the people of Zade are various, complex and unpredictable."

Dame Isabel said, "As Mr. Bickel stated, we are hardly tyros. I am sure that our good intentions will be recognized everywhere."

Cam nodded without any great conviction. "So long as you are careful, patient and discreet you should have no difficulties. I can even spare you a man to serve as interpretor. As to specific areas to visit—let me think a moment . . . The Water-people definitely. They have a well-developed music of their own. In fact music plays an important ceremonial part in their lives. And the Striads: a gentle, intelligent folk. And—who else? The Three-walkers? Probably not. They're shy and not too intelligent . . . The Mental Warriors. Yes. Don't be troubled by the name; it refers to their ritual of status by ordeal. They are a vigorous resourceful folk—probably the most intelligent of the planet."

"That should do nicely," said Dame Isabel. "What is your opinion, Bernard?"

"I agree. And we must definitely avoid the mistakes we made on Sirius Planet."

"Quite right. There will be no more tampering or adjusting; we will perform the operas precisely as they are performed at home."

Cam rose to leave. "I'll send Darwin Litchley over at once. He can take you to the districts I've mentioned, and he's an excellent linguist. Naturally I wish you all the best of luck."

He departed, and presently Darwin Litchley appeared: a short round man with a grave pink face and a bald pink scalp. "Commissioner Cam has explained your objectives," he told Dame Isabel in a portentous voice, "and while I applaud them in the abstract, I fear that problems of a lower level, the sheer ponderosity of the project, are almost certain to cause misunderstanding and difficulty."

Dame Isabel looked at him in frigid disdain. "You are a peculiarly confident man, Mr. Litchley. After weeks of meticulous planning, dedicated rehearsals and not inconsiderable expense, as well as a voyage across many miles of space, we are finally here on Zade, prepared to present our program. You now make your pessimistic enunciations, and apparently envision us reeling back in doubt and dismay, abandoning all our plans and returning to Earth."

"Madame, you misunderstand me," sputtered Litchley. "I merely hoped to present a realistic picture, in order that you should have no reason to reproach me later for irresponsibility. The peoples of Zade, while intelligent, are rather narrow in their perspective, and some are both uncertain and unreliable, and even volatile."

"Very well; you have made your point. Now let us examine the maps which I see you have brought."

Darwin Litchley gave a stiff nod, unfolded a Mercator projection of the single continent. "We are here." He indicated a point to the south and east. "Mr. Cam probably described the extreme diversity of the local aborigines, and I believe he recommended that you visit the Striads, the Water-folk and the Mental Warriors. I might have made other recommendations, but be that as it may. The Striads of the Tercera Zone—" he tapped the map "—are perhaps as good as any to visit first, and undoubtedly they are a picturesque folk."

While the *Phoebus* slid majestically across the black-orange and lime-green rain-forest, Darwin Litchley gave a brief description of the Striads.

"The folk of this planet are biologically more flexible than the people of Earth, for while all are of the same basic stock, the physical, as well as the psychological variations among them are quite extreme. The Striads, for instance, have adapted remarkably to their special circumstances. The Tercera Zone is a region of considerable volcanic activity; there are extensive hot springs and puddles of boiling mud, which the Striads use to build their castles. They are a mild people, and highly expert in the use of sound, which they project from an organ unique to them."

Ahead the rain-forest dwindled to a parkland of black bamboo-like trees and great balls of orange fluff. In the distance a line of gray mountains raised into the sky, and Darwin Litchley indicated a drift of floating mist. "That's the thermal area. Look close and you'll see the Striad cities rising out of the steam."

A few minutes later the tall fortress-like dwelling of the Striads could be seen: heavy-walled buildings of six or seven stories constructed of colored mud.

On a flat field in front of the city the *Phoebus* landed. Immediately a group of several dozen Striads stepped forth from an iron gate. Darwin Litchley, with Dame Isabel, Bernard Bickel and Roger, alighted and waited for the approach of the Striads.

They were definitely a humanoid race, tall, thin in arms and legs, but with massive ridged chests. The skins were copper-red with a glossy green sheen; the heads were tall and thin and covered with a black feathery growth; they wore shirts of coarse cloth, bronze shoulder ornaments, leaving the massive chest and the ridged shallow pit of their sound-diaphragm bare. Halting a few yards from the ship they stood rigid. Their diaphragms contracted, jerked, to emit a single soft explosion of ceremonial greeting.

Darwin Litchley spoke in a harsh language which seemed all friccatives and throat-clearings; the Striads replied after a brief consultation among themselves.

Litchley turned to Dame Isabel. "They will be happy to attend a musical performance. I must say I'm rather surprised. They're quite shy, and they've seen very few Earth people—half a dozen commercial missions, perhaps. When do you wish to stage your first performance?"

"Is tomorrow too soon?"

Darwin Litchley made the inquiry, then informed Dame Isabel that the time she had specified was quite suitable. Meanwhile the Earth folk were made welcome to the city. Litchley indicated a few simple taboos which should be observed: no entry into the buildings, no objects tossed into the thermal springs, no carousing or extravagant behavior; no special attentiveness to children, which according to Litchley were regarded as parasites and frequently eaten. When Dame Isabel expressed horror, Darwin Litchley laughed. "It is no more than tit for tat. The children retaliate by pushing the adults into the boiling springs." With Darwin Litchley's precepts in mind most of the company wandered the Striad city during the afternoon and evening. In wonder they saw the lakes of seething mud: the largest mustard-yellow; others of red, gray, chocolate brown. From this mud the tall buildings were built, and the Earth people watched in fascination as the Striads projected beams of sound and ultra-sonic vibration from their diaphragms to crack, stir or compact the mud, in its various stages of usefulness.

The Earth-people seemed to have made a good impression. A spokesman for the Striads invited the group to a banquet. After a hurried consultation with Dame Isabel, Darwin Litchley declined with thanks, stating that the group was accustomed to fasting on the eve of a musical performance.

On the following morning Globe C was opened, the central mast and canopy erected to form a theater. For the Striads Dame Isabel had selected *The Magic Flute,* and with the fiasco at Sirius Settlement fresh in mind, she had resolved that there would be no tampering or alteration. The audience would see and hear the opera precisely as it was performed on Earth. "After all," Dame Isabel told Bernard Bickel, "it smacks somehow of condescension to make these unpleasant little compromises. Our purpose is to bring the out-world folk our music as we know it, in all its power and majesty, not in some paltry bowdlerized version which the composer himself would be unable to recognize."

"Precisely my point of view," said Bernard Bickel. "I haven't noticed any manifestation of music among these Striads, but they seem, on the whole, a courteous and creative people. Perhaps you've observed the murals above the gate executed in various colors of mud?"

"Indeed; highly impressive. I must remind Roger to make photographs, which is the ostensible reason for his presence aboard the ship."

"He certainly does not appear to be enjoying himself," said Bernard Bickel. "In my opinion his nose is out of joint because Captain Gondar has been monopolizing Miss Roswyn."

Dame Isabel compressed her mouth. "I cannot consider the matter without becoming indignant, especially since we cannot dispense with Captain Gondar, who has, as you point out, taken the young creature under his wing."

Bernard Bickel shrugged. "It seems no great matter to

anyone but Roger. She keeps pretty well out of everyone's way; it's hard to imagine anyone being less obtrusive."

"I should hope so," sniffed Dame Isabel.

* * * * * * *

The hour designated as curtain time approached. The singers were in costume; the orchestra, after a good lunch and a saunter back and forth in front of the ship, had repaired to the orchestra pit where they sorted out scores and exchanged good-natured banter.

From the tall city of colored mud came the Striads, stalking as before with immense dignity and seriousness. They entered the theater and seated themselves without self-consciousness or hesitancy. Dame Isabel looked from the empty seats to the city—but no more Striads were on the way.

She summoned Darwin Litchley. "Is this all the audience we are to expect? I don't believe more than a hundred are in the theater."

"I'll make inquiries," Darwin Litchley went to speak to one of the Striads, then returned frowning to Dame Isabel. "He says this will be the entire audience: they are all individuals of responsibility—something like aldermen, I suppose—fully authorized to make whatever decisions are necessary."

Dame Isabel shook her head fretfully. "I can't say that I understand."

"Nor I," said Litchley. "Still it is probably best to stage the opera before a group like this, which at least is the elite of the city."

"This is probably the explanation," said Bernard Bickel. "I have noticed a similar situation elsewhere: a kind of cultural aristocracy which alone is privileged to explore the esthetic mysteries."

Dame Isabel peered in at the stiffly erect audience, who already were giving careful attention to the sounds of the orchestra tuning. "A rule of the artists, so to speak? A pleasant concept, certainly . . . Well, we must proceed."

Sir Henry Rixon mounted the podium. He bowed to the

audience, raised his baton: the orchestra produced the three solemn brass chords of the adagio preamble. The audience sat transfixed.

The curtain rose; Tomino came forth pursued by a serpent, and so went the performance. Dame Isabel was delighted with the concentrated attentiveness of the audience. They sat motionless, wincing approval from time to time, especially at Ada Francini's second act display of her F *in altissima*.

The opera ended; the cast came forth to bow. The audience rose slowly to their feet and for the first time conferred with each other. There seemed a certain amount of dissension, and ignoring orchestra and singers, the Striads left the theater to continue their discussion on the open ground.

Dame Isabel came forth, smiling graciously to all sides, followed by Bernard Bickel and Darwin Litchley. She marched up to the Striads. "What is your opinion of our wonderful music?" she asked brightly, and Darwin Litchley translated.

A spokesman for the group replied, and Litchley looked a trifle puzzled.

"What does he say?" asked Dame Isabel.

Litchley looked frowningly toward the Striads. "He is asking as to availability."

" 'Availability ?' I don't understand!"

"Nor I." Litchley made further inquiry and the Striad responded at length.

Darwin Litchley's eyebrows rose. He started to speak, then shrugged helplessly and turned to Dame Isabel. "There seems to be a slight mistake, a certain degree of misunderstanding," he said. "I mentioned that the Striads were familiar with Earth only through an occasional commercial mission?"

"Yes, yes!"

"They seem to have mistaken the *Phoebus* for a similar mission, and came to the performances in this frame of mind." Darwin Litchley hesitated, then spoke out in a rush. "They are not unduly impressed. They state that they need no trombones or violins, their diaphragms being adequate in this respect, but they are willing to place a firm order for two oboeists and a coloratura."

"Good heavens!" declared Dame Isabel. She turned an indignant glance toward the patiently attentive Striads. "You may tell them—"

Bernard Bickel stepped forward. "Tell them," he said smoothly, "that unfortunately these particular items are much in demand and that we cannot promise delivery at any time in the immediate future."

The Striads heard Darwin Litchley with patience and courtesy, then turned and marched slowly back toward their city. In disgust Dame Isabel ordered the theater struck, and the *Phoebus* moved to the lands of the Water-people.

* * * * * * *

A slow river flowing from the rain-forest wandered first west, then north, then south-west, and finally entered a great inland sea, traversing a delta perhaps fifty miles long and as many wide. Here the Water-people made their homes, evolving into a racial type so different from the Striads as to suggest a different race of beings. They were smaller than the Striads and supple as seals; their diaphragms were atrophied, or perhaps had never developed; in color they were a pallid gray. Their heads were rounder; the black feathery crown of the Striads were represented by a few limp strands of black-green fiber. They were much more numerous than the Striads and much more nervously active. They had altered their environment to a considerable extent, creating an astounding complexity of canals, ponds, levees, floating islands, upon and around which they either swam, poled frail scows, or propelled barges heaped with bundles and bales. In the whole area there was no single large city, merely innumerable villages of grass and reed huts. In the center of the delta, on an island roughly a mile in diameter, rose a pagoda-like tower constructed of timber, woven fiber, red-enameled panels.

Darwin Litchley had discussed the Water-folk with

Dame Isabel and Bernard Bickel at some length. "You may not find these people as cordial or as gracious as the Striads; in fact, they are inclined to a cool detachment which can very easily be interpreted as dislike. But this is not the case, nor do the Water-people lack emotional depth. But they are extremely conservative and suspicious of innovation. You may wonder why Commissioner Cam suggested you visit the Water-people, but the answer is simple. They have a highly developed music, in a tradition at least ten thousand years old."

"Well, well," said Dame Isabel with a plaintive sigh, "I am glad to come upon a people who at least know the meaning of the word 'music.' "

"No fear on that score," said Darwin Litchley. "They are true experts; all have absolute pitch; they will recognize offhand any chord you can play in any of its inversions."

"This is good news indeed," said Dame Isabel. "I don't suppose they maintain orchestras similar to our own?"

"Not precisely. Every adult is a musician of sorts, and from birth has been assigned a definite part in the ceremonial fugues, which he will play upon the instrument hereditary to his family."

"Interesting!" declared Dame Isabel. "Will we have an opportunity to hear any of the music?"

Darwin Litchley pursed his lips dubiously. "As to that, I can't say. The Water-folk are neither unhospitable nor hostile, but they are a peculiar people, as you will see for yourself, and must be taken on their own terms. I know them fairly well, and they know me—but as far as any warmth or welcome or even display of recognition—you'll see none at all. Still, you wanted to meet a musically sophisticated people and here they are."

"If they are as you say," said Dame Isabel, "I fancy we can show them something they haven't seen before. What do you suggest, Bernard?"

Bernard Bickel considered. "Rossini, perhaps: *The Barber of Seville?*"

"The idea has merit; there is a certain rollicking quality

to the work to capture the fancy of such as the Water-folk."

The *Phoebus* alighted on the island, near the pagoda-like tower, which Darwin Litchley identified as the Repository of Archives. He characterized the social system of the Water-folk as a series of paradoxes and confusions which not even the most earnest ethnologist had yet resolved. In the largest sense, each activity and phase of life seemed to be regulated and codified, and subject to the scrutiny of a series of tribunes and monitors.

Still discussing the eccentricities of the Water-folk, Dame Isabel, Darwin Litchley and Bernard Bickel descended the off ramp. Already waiting was a delegation of Water-folk, the spokesman for whom demanded the purpose of the visit.

Litchley replied in detail, and the delegation departed. "We must wait," Litchley told Dame Isabel. "They have gone to notify the Musical Commissioner."

This person arrived an hour later, with another whom he introduced as the Regional Monitor. They listened to Darwin Litchley with close attention, then the Commissioner spoke a few careful sentences which Litchley translated. "He asks the traditional background of the music you plan to—to—" he hesitated. "I can't think of a corresponding word. Launch? Promulgate? Yes. He wants to know something of the music you plan to promulgate."

"There is nothing to tell," said Dame Isabel. "It is a pleasant opera, with no explicit social message, merely a vehicle for a great deal of delightful music. We are here from sheer altruism, to share our music with him and his people."

Darwin Litchley translated, listened, turned back to Dame Isabel. "When do you propose to promulgate the music, for how long, and on how many occasions?"

"That will depend on how well we are received," replied Dame Isabel craftily. "If our program seems to give pleasure to the audience we might present several performances. If not, we will depart. It is as simple as that. Our first program will depend on the availability of an audience—which I shouldn't imagine would be difficult to find."

There were other words, and Darwin Litchley told Dame Isabel, "You may present your first program tomorrow."

"Very well," said Dame Isabel crisply. "Tomorrow it is, at three hours after noon."

* * * * * * *

In the morning the theater was assembled by the now adept crew. At two the cast assumed costumes and make-up; at two-thirty the musicians gathered in the orchestra pit.

As yet no sign of the prospective audience had evidenced itself. Dame Isabel went out to scan the countryside with a worried frown, but on all sides life seemed to proceed at its wonted pace and direction.

Ten minutes to three: still no audience.

At three o'clock precisely, the Regional Monitor whom they had met on the previous day appeared carrying a flat box. He was alone. With a brief salute for Dame Isabel, Bernard Bickel and Darwin Litchley, he marched into the theater, seated himself, opened his box from which he took paper, ink and brush and arranged all in a convenient position.

From the entrance Dame Isabel inspected him dubiously. "He's evidently come to see the opera."

Bernard Bickel made a survey of the island. "There isn't a sign of anyone else."

Dame Isabel turned to Litchley. "Find out when we may expect the audience to appear."

Litchley conferred with the monitor, returned to Dame Isabel. "He *is* the audience. He is a trifle irritated that the performance has not started on time."

"We can't play to a single individual!" protested Dame Isabel. "Did you explain that to him?"

"Well—yes. I pointed out that we were expecting rather more of a crowd, but he states that he is required to make a preliminary survey, to study and assess the performance before the population at large could risk a submission to possibly disturbing sounds. This, he says, is his duty."

Dame Isabel snapped her jaw shut; for a moment it was touch-and-go whether *The Barber of Seville* would be submitted for approval or not.

Bernard Bickel spoke in his most soothing voice, "I suppose we must expect arbitrary regulations wherever we go, especially on the more highly developed worlds. There is not much we can do about it; we must either accommodate ourselves to local custom or leave."

Dame Isabel nodded a peevish acquiescence. "I suppose you are right; however when idealistic people such as ourselves spend our talents and our money to provide this wonderful experience, it does seem that the people who will benefit might display appreciation. It is not effusiveness I want, but only some small acknowledgment; then I would be content. I do not believe—" she broke off as the monitor approached. He spoke and Litchley translated: "He is impatient for the program to commence; he notes that we are already nineteen minutes late."

Dame Isabel threw up her hands. "I do what I must." She signaled to Sir Henry Rixon, who glanced in surprise out across the expanse of benches, empty except for the attentive monitor. He looked questioningly once more to Dame Isabel, who gave him another signal. Sir Henry raised his baton. The first notes of the overture sounded and *The Barber of Seville* was under way.

The performance, played against the total non-resilience of the monitor, was not the most vivacious of anyone's experience, but on the other hand the virtuosity of the cast preserved it from becoming the empty shell, the sheer going-through-the-motions which it might well have been.

During the performance the monitor sat attentive, showing neither pleasure nor disapproval, making no motion other than an occasional taking of notes with brush and ink.

The final ensemble yielded to the ultimate orchestral chord; the curtain dropped. Dame Isabel, Bernard Bickel and Litchley turned to the monitor, who was making a few final notes. Then he rose to his feet, started for the exit. Darwin Litchley did not need Dame Isabel's bark of instructions to spring forward. There was a lengthy colloquy by the exit, until Dame Isabel broke in to inquire the nature of the monitor's judgments.

Darwin Litchley spoke laboriously. "He's unfavorably impressed; this essentially is his reaction."

"*What*?" demanded Dame Isabel. "And why is this?"

The monitor, seeming to divine the nature of Dame Isabel's exclamation, spoke to Litchley, who translated. "He has noticed a large number of clumsy mistakes. The costumes are unsuitable for the climate. Now he is making technical objection . . . The singers—hmm: a word I don't understand—*bgrassik*. Hmm. Whatever it means it's something the singers do incorrectly when attempting to—another unfamiliar phrase: *thelu gy shlrama* during orchestral implications, which result in faulty *ghark jissu*, whatever that is. 'Implications' might mean overtones . . . The chord sequences—no, that can't be what he means; chord sequences wouldn't move from north to west." He listened to the monitor, who now was reading from his notes. "The original antiphony was incomplete . . . The *thakal skth hg* were too close to the *brga skth gz*, and neither were of standard texture . . . He found the duet about halfway through interesting because of the unusual but legitimate *grsgk y thgssk trg*. He complains that the musicians sit too statically. He thinks that they should move—hop or jump if they will—in order to blend the music. The work is wild, undisciplined, with too much incorrect—substratum? Perhaps he means legato. In any event he cannot recommend the work to his people until these flaws are overcome."

Dame Isabel shook her head in complete disbelief. "It is clear that he completely misunderstands our purposes. Ask him to sit down—I will send in for tea."

The monitor acquiesced; Dame Isabel settled herself

beside him and for an hour, with occasional interpolations from Bernard Bickel, carefully explained the history, philosophy and structure of classical Earth music in general and grand opera in particular. The monitor listened politely and even took an occasional note. "Now," said Dame Isabel, "We will stage another performance—let's think . . . *Tristan und Isolde* will be taxing but I think it is apropos, in that it affords a notable contrast in style and form. Bernard, please have the Wagner people into their costumes: *Tristan und Isolde* in twenty minutes. Roger, notify Sir Henry and Andrei. Quickly now, we must convince this monitor that we are not the dunces he takes us for!"

The musicians returned to the pit, the violinists massaged their fingers, the trumpeters applied salve to their lips; and it was a tribute to the virtuosity of the group and the dynamic qualities of Sir Henry's baton that the Prelude came forth in all its ineffable bitter-sweet passion.

During the performance, Dame Isabel, Bernard Bickel and Darwin Litchley sat beside the silver-skinned monitor, explaining to the best of their powers the subtleties of the spiritual conflict which unfolded before them. The monitor made no comments, and perhaps paid no great heed to the commentary; as before he brushed enigmatic marks upon his notepad.

The performance came to an end; Isolde sang the *Liebestod*; her voice faded into echo; up through the weft of orchestral sound came the plangent voice of the oboe, pronouncing the great theme of magic and woe . . . The curtain fell.

Dame Isabel turned to Darwin Litchley. "Now then! I hope he is satisfied!"

The monitor spoke in his husky consonanted language; Litchley listened with a slack jaw. Dame Isabel stuttered and would have leapt to her feet but for Bernard Bickel's restraining hand.

"He is still—somewhat critical," said Litchley in a hollow voice. "He says he understands something of our point of view, but this is no excuse for poor music. He specifically objects to what he terms the stifling monotony of our chord progressions: he says it would drive an audience less broadminded than himself mad with boredom. He finds our music as reiterative as a children's chant, with every modulation, every new theme, every recurrence of an old theme, expressed with a pedantic and unimaginative predictability."

Dame Isabel closed her eyes. The monitor had once more gained his feet. "Sit down," she said in a harsh strained voice. "Bernard: we will now perform *Wozzeck*."

Bernard Bickel's handsome gray eyebrows rose into astonished arcs. "*Wozzeck*? Now?"

"At once. Please inform Andrei and Sir Henry."

Bernard Bickel, looking back over his shoulder, went off to do her bidding. He presently returned. "The company is fatigued," he said uncertainly. "They haven't eaten since noon; Hermilda Warn complains of sore feet, as do Christina Reite and Ephraim Zerner. The first violinist states that he will be forced to play in gloves because of a blister."

Dame Isabel said in a cold quiet voice: "The performance of *Wozzeck* will get under way in twenty minutes. The singers will change costume, but need not concern themselves with fresh make-up. Distribute lozenges to any who complain of hoarseness; those with sore feet would be well-advised to change into casual foot-gear."

Bernard Bickel departed backstage; the musicians presently filed back into the orchestra pit. There were surly mutters, much slamming around of scores. The first violinist ostentatiously drew white cotton gloves over his hands; the second trombonist blew a vulgar *glissando*.

Sir Henry Rixon sternly rapped the podium with his baton.

Wozzeck! And Dame Isabel watched the monitor with a small secret smile, as if to say, "You think our chords are obvious, do you? Analyze a few of these."

It was a weary but paradoxically triumphant company which brought *Wozzeck* to its dire finale. The monitor consulted his notes with studious attention; but Dame Isabel insisted that all repair to the saloon for a cup of tea and a biscuit. When they were seated she fixed the monitor with a questioning look which was almost a challenge. "Now then?"

The monitor spoke; Darwin Litchley translated in a dull voice. "I cannot recommend tendentious, provocative, or persuasive matter for the attention of the Waterfolk. This last improvisation is clever but desperate, and as a final remark, I would recommend that those musicians entrusted with the *bsg rgassik* listen for the introductory *slfks* from the air-swish."

" 'Air-swish?' "

"He refers to Sir Henry's baton. He can hear the sounds it makes passing through the air and believes it to be a musical instrument."

Dame Isabel said in an icy voice, "He is clearly a cretin. You may inform him that our patience is exhausted, that we resolutely refuse to perform before a group so tone-deaf, so arbitrary and opinionated as the Waterfolk."

Darwin Litchley cautiously rendered a version of the remarks; the monitor listened without interest. He bent over his pad and seemed to be performing calculations. He spoke to Darwin Litchley, who blinked, then hesitantly translated. "He has set his fee at—"

"His 'fee?' " demanded Dame Isabel in a voice which cracked with emotion. "What an astonishing impudence! Order him off the ship instantly!"

Darwin Litchley spoke in a conciliatory voice, "Local usage is such that the monitor must make a charge for his expertise. Six hundred flashlight batteries may seem—"

"What in the world are you talking about?" demanded Dame Isabel. "What is this talk of 'flashlight batteries?' "

Litchley smiled weakly. "Flashlight batteries are the local medium of exchange—at least for transactions between Earth people and the aborigines."

Dame Isabel said clearly and distinctly: "Inform this creature that he will be paid nothing, in flashlight batteries or otherwise. Explain that I consider his attitude highly insolent, that he has imposed not only upon me, but also Mr. Bickel and indeed the whole company: if there is any paying of flashlight batteries to be done, it is he who should pay us. Inform him that we are tired and that he may now go. Roger! Inform Captain Gondar that the theater may be disassembled at once!"

The monitor had not moved from his seat. Dame Isabel gave him an incredulous stare. "What now?"

Darwin Litchley said in a flustered voice, "He tells me that he miscalculated; in addition to the six hundred batteries, there is a surcharge for compositions performed in more than three tonalities, which puts an added strain on the critical faculties. The surcharge in the case of the first two works is fifty flashlight batteries apiece, in the case of *Wozzeck* he estimates a hundred and fifty. To a total of eight hundred and fifty."

"Tell him to leave. We will pay him nothing."

Litchley and the monitor engaged in a short conversation; then Litchley told Dame Isabel, "He says that if he is not paid he will discharge the contents of his spore-sac into the air, which will infect the *Phoebus* with approximately ten million infant Water-people, more or less similar to himself."

Dame Isabel opened her mouth to speak, closed it again. She turned to Bernard Bickel. "I suppose we must pay?"

"Yes," said Bernard Bickel sadly. "We must pay."

"We do not have that many flashlight batteries aboard ship," Dame Isabel told Darwin Litchley. "What shall we do then?"

"Let me call the Commissioner Cam; he will send out a flyer with the requisite sum."

An hour later the flyer arrived. The monitor was paid his batteries and without further ado departed the *Phoebus*.

"This is the most exasperating situation I can remember," said Dame Isabel. "How is it possible for any set of intelligent individuals to be so arrogantly narrow-minded?"

Bernard Bickel laughed. "If you have traveled space as much as I, you would be surprised by nothing. And as we realized long ago, for every one of our triumphs we will encounter disappointment or incomprehension."

"Perhaps I expect too much. Still—" Dame Isabel shook her head, poured herself a cup of tea. "I suppose I am far too optimistic and trusting. I wonder if I will ever learn?" She sighed. "But we can only do our best; once we compromise with our ideals, all is lost. Mr. Litchley, these Mental Warriors you are taking us to—I hope they are not the same finicky sort as the Water-people?"

Litchley said tentatively, "I do not know them as well as I know the Water-people, but by all reports they are outgoing and hearty, if perhaps not so subtle as one or two other tribes of Zade."

"I am glad to hear that," said Dame Isabel with a grateful sigh. "I am bored with calculating folk who can think of nothing but criticism and flashlight batteries. My word, but I am tired. I think I will retire. Bernard, please see to it that the theater is stowed in good order. We will depart first thing in the morning."

* * * * *

The *Phoebus* slid west and north across the splendid scenery of Zade. Mountains and plains passed below, with an occasional town or village and one city of tall stone spires. This, according to Darwin Litchley, was inhabited by a people who had the faculty of seeing demons which were invisible to other folk. They were a gentle responsive race, but—so he stated in answer to Dame Isabel's query—not to be considered in the light of a prospective audience: if they perceived, or thought to perceive, spectres among the company, their cries of horror would be certain to disrupt the performance.

They crossed over a jungle of the many-colored trees characteristic to the planet, approached a great massif of schists, gneisses and other metamorphic rock, and presently came to the land of the Mental Warriors: a region of dark fractured stone, chasms and abysses, peaks, scarps and crags. The principal city—hardly more than a large town—occupied the center of a fairly level plateau. Nearby was a complex of foundries, smelting sheds and forges, surrounded by heaps of slag and ort. Darwin Litchley described the Mental Warriors as proficient miners and smelters, suppliers of iron and copper to the whole continent. "Don't be perturbed by their appearance or manner," he said. "They are a stern harsh folk, but by no means savage or unreliable. I am not too familiar with their culture, but they are famous among the other races of Zade for their pageants and spectacular demonstrations, and they are said to be open-minded people. If we conduct ourselves with a normal regard for their sensibilities, I am sure that we will be treated with punctilious courtesy."

Captain Gondar landed the *Phoebus* on an open area near the town; Dame Isabel, Bernard Bickel and Darwin Litchley stepped down the ramp and awaited the arrival of a local deputation. This was not long in arriving.

As Darwin Litchley had predicted, their appearance was by no means engaging. They were a tall crag-featured people, with torsos sheathed in black segmented chitin. They seemed of remarkable physical strength, and wore garments which would have weighed down an Earthman: iron sandals, a kilt of iron tablets bound with bronze wire, bronze and iron epaulette-like shoulder coverings from which depended strings of silver beads. They wore no headgear, and their scalps were corrugated with two-inch ridges of black chitin. Halting, they directed upon the group from the *Phoebus* a scrutiny of intense concentration, assessing and gauging every aspect of the visitors' being.

One of them spoke in a heavy harsh voice which seemed all broad vowels. Darwin Litchley listened with care, and responded rather haltingly. The Mental Warrior made another statement; Litchley turned to Dame Isabel and Bernard Bickel. "He wants to know the reason for our visit, or so I gather. I told him that you were just arrived from Earth, that you had heard of the Mental Warriors and wanted to see them. A little flattery never comes amiss."

"By no means," declared Bernard Bickel. "Tell them that their sterling qualities are known over all the human universe, that we have come to pay our respects, and stage a performance for their benefit."

Darwin Litchley translated, using the heavy groaning language as best he could. The Mental Warriors listened with brooding attention, then drew apart to confer among themselves, darting the Earth-people glances of wary calculation.

They returned slowly to where the three from the *Phoebus* waited. The spokesman made an inquiry: "You state that our reputation is known across the universe?"—so Litchley translated.

"Yes, indeed," replied Bernard Bickel, and Litchley conveyed the message.

"You have come here with no other purpose than to provide this 'performance?' "

"That is the case. Our company includes some of the most talented artists of Earth."

The Mental Warriors withdrew again, and seemed to fall into dissension. Finally agreement was reached; the Mental Warriors returned; the spokesman uttered a set of heavy fateful phrases.

Litchley translated. "They accept the invitation; they will send a delegation of their bravest and wisest notables—"

" 'Bravest and wisest?' " inquired Dame Isabel in puzzlement. "What a strange way to speak!"

"That seems to be the essence of the remark. He makes a condition, however: all of us aboard the *Phoebus* in our turn attend a performance staged in their arena by their specially trained troupe."

After a brief pause and an uncertain look toward the Mental Warriors, Dame Isabel said, "I see no reason why we should not accept the invitation . . . In fact, it would seem churlish to refuse. Do you not agree, Bernard?"

Bickel rubbed his chin, looked doubtfully toward the

grimly attentive autochthones. "I suppose they feel a strong sense of obligation. Their rather dire attitude probably means nothing whatever."

"Is not this the very essence of cultural interchange?" inquired Dame Isabel. "Why have we come all these millions of miles if not for this very purpose?" She turned to Darwin Litchley. "We will be honored to attend their performance! Please convey as much to them."

Litchley spoke; there was some slight further conversation and the delegation returned to the city.

Dame Isabel and Bernard Bickel immediately conferred with Andrei Szinc and Sir Henry Rixon in regard to an appropriate program. Bernard Bickel, who had been impressed by the forcefulness of the Mental Warriors' character, voted for *Siegfried,* on the basis of relevance to the lives of the audience. Andrei Szinc declared for *Aida,* for which the *Phoebus* carried particularly striking sets; Sir Henry raised, then dismissed, the Decadents; Dame Isabel brought forward the idea that this particular folk, with their obviously toilsome lives, might well be diverted by something charming and carefree: *Hansel and Gretel, Die Fledermaus, Cosi Fan Tutte,* or even *Tales of Hoffman.*

Eventually *The Bartered Bride* was agreed upon; Andrei Szinc departed to put the cast through a quick rehearsal; Sir Henry went off to review the score.

The night was dark; from the forges across the plateau came an eery flicker. The air carried odors strange to the nostrils of Earth-folk, and those who had come forth to stretch their legs stayed close to the ship.

On the following day the theater was erected; the orchestra ran through the score. At the time appointed a large company of Mental Warriors marched across the plateau. Dame Isabel met them at the entrance to the theater. The spokesman came forward, indicated his fellows, and spoke. Darwin Litchley translated. "We have come, in faithful accordance with our undertaking. Once we are determined, neither persuasion, trepidation, nor second thoughts can deter us. So now we submit ourselves to your performance."

Dame Isabel uttered a short speech of welcome, then led them into the theater. With quick looks to left and right, they seated themselves in a compact group, each adopting an identical, somewhat rigid posture: torso bolt upright, arms pressed closely to the sides, feet planted close together.

Sir Henry Rixon raised his baton for the overture: the Mental Warriors as one man fixed their eyes upon him. The curtain rose on the first act; the Mental Warriors sat as if frozen; indeed they did not so much as twitch until the final curtain descended and the lights came on; even then they remained motionless, as if not certain that the performance was over. Then slowly, uncertainly, they rose to their feet, filed from the theater, exchanging puzzled comments. Dame Isabel and Bernard Bickel met them outside. The spokesman conferred with his fellows, and it seemed as if they were somewhat resentful though the dour cast of their features made any such judgment uncertain.

Dame Isabel approached. "Did you enjoy the performance?"

The spokesman said in his most resonant voice, "My people are neither exercised nor taxed; is this the most vigorous performance you are able to provide? Are the folk of Earth so listless?"

Darwin Litchley translated; Dame Isabel was surprised at the question. "We have dozens of operas in our repertory, all different. We conferred at length last night and decided that you might enjoy something light and not too rigorous or tragic."

The Mental Warrior drew himself stiffly erect. "Do you take us so lightly then? Is this our reputation across the cosmos?"

"No, no, of course not," Dame Isabel told him. "By no means!"

The Mental Warrior spoke a few brusque words to his fellows, turned back to Dame Isabel. "We will say no more of the performance. Tomorrow we will honor you with an exhibition by our trained company. You will attend?"

"Of course!" said Dame Isabel. "We are looking forward to the occasion. Will you send someone to guide us to your theater?"

"This will be done." The Mental Warriors stalked off across the plain.

Bernard Bickel shook his head. "I fear that they weren't too impressed."

Dame Isabel sighed. "Just possibly they might have preferred *Siegfried* . . . Well, we'll see. Tomorrow's performance should be very interesting, and I must remind Roger to bring along recording equipment."

* * * * *

On the day following, a few minutes after the noon meal, a pair of Mental Warriors presented themselves at the ship. Not everyone was ready; Ramona Thoxted and Cassandra Prouty at the last moment decided to change from afternoon frocks to somewhat more casual clothes. Finally all who were going assembled outside the ship: singers, musicians, Dame Isabel, Roger, Bernard Bickel, Sir Henry, Andrei Szinc, and a number of the crew. Neither Captain Gondar nor Madoc Roswyn was among the group, and Roger felt an agonized pang at the thought of the two together. Someone else seemed to have similar feelings: Logan de Appling, the personable young astrogator. He strode back and forth nervously toward the debarkation ramp, and when neither Madoc Roswyn nor Captain Gondar appeared, he abruptly marched back aboard ship.

At last all were on hand; in a festive mood they set off across the plateau. Forgotten were little disagreements and jealousies; various small cliques had temporarily dissolved, and it was a good-natured group which walked chattering and chaffering to the local theater Ramona Thoxted and Cassandra Prouty congratulated themselves on their decision to wear casual clothes; the occasion clearly was not at all formal. Even Dame Isabel seemed caught up in the spirit of good cheer, and made jocular references to the book Roger was supposed to be writing.

They passed behind the city, descended a wide stone-paved path and found themselves in a natural amphitheater. The walls were steep and the seats were all on the floor of the enclosure: stone cylinders arranged in concentric circles.

Dame Isabel examined the amphitheater with lively interest. "They pay not even lip-service to luxury," she observed to Bernard Bickel. "The seats, or pedestals, whatever you call them, appear absolutely uncomfortable. But I suppose we must take things as we find them."

Bernard Bickel indicated the iron trusswork overhead. "Evidently for special effects, or perhaps lighting arrangements."

Dame Isabel looked about. "A strange sort of theater: where is the stage? Where do the musicians sit?"

Bernard Bickel chuckled. "In my peregrinations across the galaxy, I've learned to be surprised at nothing, not even theaters without stages."

"Yes, we must not be too parochial . . . Well, I believe I will sit here. Roger, you take that seat or pedestal, whatever, and Mr. Litchley, you sit there, beside Roger, so that if necessary you can make interpretive comments into the recording apparatus."

The company disposed itself about the amphitheater with jocular remarks back and forth.

The individual who had acted as spokesman for the Mental Warriors appeared. He clanked across the stone floor of the arena to Dame Isabel. He spoke and Darwin Litchley translated: "You have kept your word; you have not departed the planet."

"No, naturally not," declared Dame Isabel. "Such an act would have been highly ungenerous."

At the translation, the Mental Warrior gave a brief jerk of his head. "You are a strange folk; but certainly one to be respected."

"Thank you very much," said Dame Isabel, extremely

pleased, and Bernard Bickel added a smiling nod of acknowledgment.

The Mental Warrior departed the arena. Silence persisted for two minutes, and was broken by the chime of a great gong. This was the signal for a set of astonishing and harrowing circumstances. Jets of flame thrust up from the floor; iron rails fell from above to crash into the aisles between pedestals. Six razor-edged pendulums were released from above, to swing back and forth. A siren screamed, and was answered by another; a great boulder toppled down, to be caught by a chain inches above the heads of the audience. The fire jets thrust out horizontally, then vertically, and down from the trusses dropped chunks of red-hot iron . . . After two minutes and fourteen seconds the company was screaming, fainting, giving way to various styles of hysteria.

Abruptly the performance was terminated. The Mental Warriors appeared on the truss-work and to the side of the arena. They emitted hoots, cat-calls, harsh cries of scorn. Darwin Litchley later remembered something of their comments: "What sort of pusillanimity is this?" And "We sat through three hours of your worst and never flinched!" And "The folk of Earth are weaklings indeed!"

In a disorganized straggle the group returned to the *Phoebus*. Dame Isabel gave instant orders to strike the theater and depart with the most expedition possible.

The *Phoebus* flew back to Earthtown, discharged Darwin Litchley, and at once put off into space.

Chapter Nine

THE FOLLOWING day, with Phi Orionis a near-anonymous glitter astern, Dame Isabel had regained enough composure to be able to discuss the events on the plateau with Bernard Bickel. "I dislike to impute malevolence to anyone, and somehow I cannot read animus into that terrible set of circumstances."

"Probably not," said Bernard Bickel wanly. "A misunderstanding, more than likely . . . Faulty communication. What a farcical chap, that Litchley! Utterly incompetent!"

"I am inclined to agree with you," said Dame Isabel. "Only a completely inept person could have mistranslated 'performance' for 'ordeal;' or 'invitation' for 'challenge.' "

"To do the fellow justice," mused Bernard Bickel, "he frankly admitted his shakiness in the language. And it sounded like nothing else than a herd of dying sheep."

Captain Gondar had entered the saloon; now he joined them. He was not looking well; there were dark shadows under his eyes, and his normally sallow skin showed a yellowish undertone. Perhaps not too tactfully, Dame Isabel commented upon his appearance. "You should take more exercise, Captain Gondar. Even in this age of biological miracles, we must cooperate by keeping the blood flowing in our veins."

Captain Gondar gave an uninterested nod. "A short while ago I mentioned a civilized and cultured planet—"

"Yes, I remember distinctly. To visit the planet would entail an onerous detour."

"Some small distance, perhaps," Gondar conceded. "A matter of veering off into Hydra. You quite properly pointed out that if our ultimate destination were in Cetus—and I am not completely convinced as to the wisdom of this—"

"What!" exclaimed Dame Isabel. "This is the principal motive for the tour, our visit to Rlaru! We must never for an instant think otherwise!"

Captain Gondar massaged his foreread. "Of course. But this planet in Hydra is no less advanced than Rlaru. The people might even agree to send a troupe of musicians to Earth, on the order of the Ninth Company."

Dame Isabel glanced toward Bernard Bickel, who gave his head a skeptical shake. She spoke in an even voice. "Captain, this planet no doubt merits a visit. But we have a schedule judiciously, even laboriously, arrived at, and we simply cannot pursue every will-o-the-wisp that offers itself." She held up her hand as Captain Gondar started to speak. "There is another completely compelling reason why we cannot make this sidetrip. Our immediate destination is Skylark. If we can bring a single sparkle of gayety to the unfortunates confined there, all the effort and expense of the tour will be justified. Skylark is in Eridanus, and only a slight change of course will take us into Cetus, so you can see that a detour is out of the question."

Captain Gondar stared at her, his face hollow and desolate. "If I were you," said Dame Isabel, not unkindly, "I would consult Dr. Shand and ask him for a tonic; I feel you must be driving yourself too hard."

Captain Gondar made a harsh inarticulate noise. He jumped to his feet and left the saloon.

"What a strange fellow!" said Dame Isabel. "Whatever can be his trouble?"

Bernard Bickel smiled. "In my opinion Captain Gondar's little *affaire de coeur* is not proceeding with 'rose-petal felicity,' as Carveth puts it."

Dame Isabel shook her head indignantly. "What a heartless little wretch she is! First poor Roger and now Captain Gondar!" Resolutely she reached for the notes Bernard Bickel had assembled on Eridanus BG12-IV, popularly known as 'Skylark.' "I suppose we cannot interfere in these matters." She gave her attention to the notes, but almost immediately looked up in wry reproach. "Bernard—aren't you a trifle severe?"

Bickel leaned forward in surprise. "How so?"

"After noting the physical characteristics of the planet you state, 'Skylark derives its interest mainly from the fact that during the last two hundred years it has served as a penal colony for the most depraved, unregenerate and callous criminals of the human universe.' "

Bickel shrugged. "Skylark is notoriously the end of the line."

"I refuse to think in those terms," said Dame Isabel. "Many of these 'criminals' are quite simply victims of destiny." And she glanced sharply at Roger, who had wandered into the saloon.

"This is true of us all, to some extent," Bernard Bickel pointed out.

"Exactly my point! In a small way I regard the *Phoebus* as an aspect of destiny—but a beneficent aspect. If we can convince even a dozen of the convicts that they are not forgotten, not totally abandoned; if we can stimulate this dozen to make a fresh appraisal of themselves, the visit to Skylark will be a success."

"The sentiment does you credit," said Bernard Bickel, and he added, rather ruefully, "naturally I have no theoretical objection to humanitarianism."

"Of course not; please don't take me seriously. To tell the truth, I am just a bit out of sorts. Problems pile up; we have not achieved a half of our expectations, and in fact the entire company seems a trifle flat."

"The performances on Zade took a great deal out of everyone," said Bernard Bickel. "But a success or two will do a world of good."

"Captain Gondar has been acting so strangely," Dame Isabel complained. "This planet in Hydra seems almost an obsession with him. And I've had complaints that the crew has started up that awful racket again, with their tin cans and mouth-organs."

"Oh yes. The Tough Luck Jug Band." Bernard Bickel shook his head in sad disparagement. "I'll have a word with the Chief Steward."

"Please be quite definite, Bernard. We can't have everyone upset just because of the thoughtless horseplay of two or three individuals . . . Roger, I suppose you are well along with your book?" Dame Isabel spoke the last with a sardonic edge to her voice.

"I'm taking notes," said Roger sullenly. "It's a big project."

"I must point out that the woman you brought aboard has caused no end of trouble, and I hold you strictly accountable . . . What did you say, Roger?"

"I said 'fantastic!' "

" 'Fantastic?' What is fantastic?"

"I was thinking of your benevolence in regard to the criminals of Skylark."

Dame Isabel opened her mouth, shut it again—for once at a loss for words. Finally she said, "My ethical doctrine, Roger, is based upon the principles of responsibility and self-respect, for those who are capable of exemplifying these principles. One more matter, since we are approaching Skylark. For all my 'benevolence' as you term it, I am still a realist, and I plan to enjoin everyone aboard to the utmost discretion. Under no circumstances will we fraternize with the prisoners, invite them aboard the ship, offer them liquor or use anything other than the most impersonal courtesy."

"I never intended otherwise," said Roger with dignity.

"The Skylark authorities will probably issue similar regulations," said Bernard Bickel. "Skylark is not precisely a fortress or a row of dungeons, and the prisoners have a certain degree of freedom; we don't want them running off with the ship."

"Definitely not," said Dame Isabel. "But I am sure that if we use the most basic elementary caution, all will go well."

* * * * * * *

Skylark looked large in the sky; from an orbit thirty thousand miles above the planet, the *Phoebus* radioed down for landing clearance. A patrol boat eased alongside; four officials came aboard, inspected the ship, conferred for several hours with Dame Isabel and Captain Gondar. "You must realize," said the Senior Inspector, a thin gray-haired man with drooping mustaches and darting black eyes, "that Skylark bears no resemblance to the usual prison. The convicts are allowed the freedom of almost ten square miles, the full extent of the Table."

"How do you enforce discipline?" asked Dame Isabel. "It would seem that fourteen thousand desperate men, if they felt so inclined, could easily overwhelm a comparative handful of administrative personnel."

"We have our methods, never fear. I assure you they are effective. We use a great deal of electronic surveillance, and our little electric hornets are never trifled with. No, we worry more about boredom than disorder. Life here is absolutely placid."

"I should think our visit would do a great deal to raise morale," said Dame Isabel. "The prisoners must be absolutely starved for music."

The Senior Inspector chuckled. "We are not such barbarians as all that; we have several good orchestras of our own. Our population, after all, is derived from all walks of life. We have convict carpenters, plumbers, farmers and musicians. Our architects are convicts, our hospital is staffed by convicts, our chemists and agronomists are convicts. We comprise a self-contained community—a criminal civilization, one might put it. Still, we are grateful for an occasional breath of fresh air, something to distract us from our troubles, and this you have been kind enough to offer."

"Not at all," said Dame Isabel. "We are pleased to be of service. Now as to program, I propose *Turandot, Der Rosenkavalier, Cosi Fan Tutte*—a generally cheerful and amusing group. *Turandot* is a trifle macabre, but in such an extravagant fashion that no one could possibly be adversely influenced."

The Senior Inspector assured her that there need be no worries on this account. "A number of very macabre folk live among us; we are not likely to be shocked by a few theatrical extravagances."

"Excellent. Now precisely what restrictions or regulations do you wish to impose upon us?"

"Very few, really. No weapons, drugs or liquor for the prisoners, naturally. Guards will control access to the ship, and we'll want all your personnel aboard ship before dark. The prisoners are generally well-behaved, but there are erratic and undisciplined persons among us, it goes without saying. For instance, it would be highly unadvisable for any attractive young woman to wander off by herself: she might find far more hospitality than she bargained for."

Dame Isabel said stiffly, "I will pose a set of specific warnings, although I doubt if anyone aboard would be so foolish."

"One last matter: We will require an exact manifest of all your personnel, so that if you land with say, a hundred and one persons, we can be assured that exactly a hundred and one persons depart."

Captain Gondar provided the necessary list; the officials departed; the *Phoebus* swerved down to a landing.

* * * * * * *

Skylark, barely seven thousand miles in diameter, was the smallest planet yet visited by the *Phoebus*. From the vantage of the orbit the surface seemed smooth and homogeneous, mossy green in color, with a barely perceptible darkening at the poles. The green proved to be a pulsing and purulent swamp, with the penal colony on an enormous volcanic plug rearing two thousand feet into the relatively cool upper air. On the plateau the original ecology had been modified and now Earthtype vegetation dominated.

At first sight the colony seemed a rather pleasant little community; indeed the structure with an institutional look—a four-story block of concrete with impenetrex windows—was that occupied by the Governor and his staff.

Elsewhere were four neat villages, a manufacturing facility, various commissaries, offices and depots, entirely manned by the convicts. Their comings and goings seemed their own; they carried themselves without overt furtiveness, though never could they be mistaken for free men. The distinction was hard to define—possibly because the quality, blended of melancholy, obsequiousness, withdrawal, smouldering bitterness, a lack of spontaneity, manifested itself differently in each case.

Another, even more subtle characteristic might have gone unnoticed, except for the fact that all convicts wore the prison uniform: gray trousers and blue jackets. Dame Isabel, inspecting the crowd who had come to stare at the *Phoebus,* was the first to put this quality into words. "Strange," she told Bernard Bickel, "I had somehow expected a less personable group of men: repellent brutes and thugs, obvious morons, and the like. But not one of these men would attract a second glance at the most fashionable function. In fact, there is a curious uniformity to their appearance."

Bernard Bickel acknowledged the validity of the observation, but was at a loss for an explanation. "The fact that they all wear prison issue may emphasize the similarity," was his best guess.

During a second consultation with the Senior Inspector Dame Isabel raised the point again. "Is it my imagination, and no more, or is it a fact that the convicts seem to resemble one another?"

The Senior Inspector, himself a rather handsome man of medium physique with fine regular features, was somewhat surprised. "Do you really think so?"

"Yes, though it's an elusive resemblance. I notice all complexions here and all somatic types; still in some manner . . ." She paused, searching for the exact words to express the half-intuitive conviction.

The inspector suddenly chuckled. "I think I can explain. What you observe is negative rather than positive, a lack rather than a presence, which is much more difficult to define."

"This may well be true. What puzzles me is that I observe no 'criminal types,' though I will not defend the scientific validity of the term."

"Exactly. And this is a matter of which we are strongly conscious. We do not want 'criminal types' here at Skylark."

"But how in the world do you avoid them? At a penal colony for the utterly unregenerate, I would think 'criminal types' would abound!"

"We get our share," admitted the inspector. "But they are not with us long."

"You mean—they are done away with?"

"Oh no. Nothing like that. Our feeling is that 'criminal type—criminal act' is a relationship which works in both directions: that is to say, many persons, especially the highly suggestible, are compelled to act out the symbologic implications of their physiognomies. A man with a prognathous chin as he examines himself in a mirror will say, Ah, I have a strong aggressive chin! He will tend to impose this judgment upon his course of action. A person with small narrow red-rimmed eyes will be conscious of his 'shifty furtive expression;' he likewise will tend to act out this role. By doing so, of course, he reinforces the popular suppositions which initially created the symbology. Here on Skylark we are sensitive to these relationships, if for no other reason than self-interest. When we receive an individual with beady eyes, receding chin, loose-lipped mouth, an idiotic or malign expression, we process him in what we call our 'Reconstruction Laboratories,' and remove his most demoralizing flaws. I suppose that our staff—all convict, by the way—tends to standardize upon certain optimun patterns: so that you not only notice a lack of weak chins, shifty eyes and lecherous mouths, but a higher-than-normal proportion of straight noses, noble foreheads, stalwart jaws and benevolent gazes."

"Yes!" declared Dame Isabel. "This is precisely the situation. And the personalities undergo similar changes?"

"In most cases, though we are by no means a colony of idealistic philanthropists." He spoke the last with a jocular twitch of the lips.

"As a matter of fact," said Dame Isabel, "I have been wondering how so small an administrative staff controls such a large number of desperate men. The settlement must be prone to factions and cliques and—what is the term?—kangaroo courts. Not to mention sheer insubordination and riots."

The inspector acknowledged the pertinence of Dame Isabel's remarks. "All these might be troublesome without strict discipline. We control certain privileges, and of course we have one or two little tricks. One of our unique institutions is what we call a 'supervisory militia,' composed of responsible prisoners. They act as the arm of a judicial office, also staffed by prisoners. The verdicts are naturally reviewed by the governor, but he seldom interferes, even in the rare sentences of transportation."

"Transportation?" inquired Dame Isabel. "To where?"

"To the other side of the planet, the final stage of the journey by parachute."

"Into the jungle? But that must be equivalent to death."

The inspector gave a wry grimace. "We do not know for sure; none of the transported men have ever been seen again."

Dame Isabel shuddered. "I suppose that even a society of convicts must protect itself."

"Such events are extremely rare; actually there is less 'crime' here than might be found in a similar community on Earth."

Dame Isabel shook her head in wonder. "I would expect people in such grim circumstances to be completely indifferent to life or death."

The inspector smiled gently. "By no means. In a quiet way I enjoy my life: I would neither wish to be transported, nor forfeit my status."

Dame Isabel blinked. "You—you are a convict? Surely not?"

"Indeed I am," declared the inspector. "I murdered my grandmother with an axe, and since it was my second precisely identical offense—"

"Second?" asked Roger, who had wandered up a few moments previously. "Precisely identical? How could that be?"

"Everyone has two grandmothers," the inspector told him politely. "But this is all water under the bridge, and some of us—not many, but a few—make a new life for ourselves. Some of us—again not many—are transported. The rest are simply—convicts."

"All this is highly illuminating," said Dame Isabel. With a meaningful glance for Roger she added. "It is also a strong argument against idleness and libertinism, and for a career of hard and useful work."

* * * * * *

On the second day after arrival *Turandot* was performed before a packed house. *Der Rosenkavalier* and *Cosi Fan Tutte* met with equal success, to such effect that the gloom and listlessness which had threatened to demoralize the company vanished completely.

The Governor entertained the company at a buffet dinner, and his expressions of gratitude touched Dame Isabel to such an extent that she promised another three performances and asked the Governor to name his special favorites. Declaring himself partial to Verdi, he suggested *Rigoletto, La Traviata* and *Il Trovatore*. Dame Isabel wondered whether the unrelieved tragedy, no matter how unreal, might not depress the convicts. The Governor, dispelled her apprehensions. "By no means; do the blighters good to realize that someone beside themselves has troubles." He was a large stout man with a bluff manner which obviously concealed a real talent for administration.

Immediately after the Governor's dinner the Skylark Symphonic Orchestra presented a short concert in honor of the *Phoebus,* and Sir Henry Rixon delivered a speech

celebrating the universality of music. On the day following *Rigoletto* was performed, then *La Traviata,* then *Il
Trovatore,* and at every performance uniformed guards
were needed to prevent overcrowding in the theater.
Other precautions were rigidly enforced: the ship's entry-
port was guarded and every night members of the crew in
the company of administration personnel made a careful
inspection of every cubic inch of the ship.

After *Il Trovatore,* musicians and singers alike were exhausted. The audience clamored for more, and Dame Isabel, stepping before the footlights made a short speech
regretting the necessity for departure. "We have many
other worlds to visit, many other folk before whom to
perform. But be assured that we have enjoyed playing before you, and your applause has definitely been most
heartening. If we ever make another similar tour of the
stars, be assured that without fail we shall call by Skylark!"

After the performance the guards gave the ship an even
more careful scrutiny than usual. On the morrow, before
departure, there would be another search and the final
formalities.

* * * * * * *

The guards had departed the ship, to keep vigilant
watch by the entry-port, which was sealed from within
and without. Roger walked uneasily here and there: from
the bridge, through the crew's mess-hall, back to the
saloon where Madoc Roswyn sat playing cribbage with
Logan de Appling, and it was an indication of Roger's
perplexity that he hardly noticed. At last he made up his
mind. Going to Dame Isabel's cabin, he knocked on the
door.

"Yes? Who is it?"

"It's I. Roger."

The door opened; Dame Isabel looked out. "What is
the matter?"

"Can I come in for a moment? There's something I've
got to tell you."

"I'm extremely tired; Roger. Certainly tomorrow should be early enough for whatever is troubling you."

"I'm not so sure. There's something very strange going on."

"Strange? What manner of strangeness?"

Roger looked up and down the corridor. All other doors were closed, but nevertheless he lowered his voice. "You heard the orchestra tonight?"

"Yes, naturally."

"Did you notice anything well, different?"

"I did not."

"Well, I did. It's something rather trivial I suppose, but the more I think of it the stranger it seems."

"If you inform me as to what you noticed, I might be in a position to judge."

"Have you ever watched Calvin Martineau, the first oboeist?"

"With no great attention."

"He's always good for a laugh. Before he plays he shoots his cuffs, puffs out his cheeks, and makes a peculiar face."

"Mr. Martineau," said Dame Isabel, "is an excellent musician. The oboe, in case you are unaware of the fact, is a difficult instrument."

"I imagine it must be. Tonight—I'm not sure about last night—the man playing first oboe was not Martineau."

Dame Isabel shook her head in disparagement. "Please, Roger, I am very tired indeed."

"But this is important!" cried Roger. "If the first oboeist is not Mr. Martineau—who is he?"

"Do you think Sir Henry would be unaware of this strange circumstance?"

Roger shook his head doggedly. "He looks like Mr. Martineau. But his ears aren't so big. Mr. Martineau's ears were quite noticeable—"

"And this is the basis for your alarm?"

"Oh no. I watched him play. He sat still. He didn't make any peculiar faces. He didn't shoot his cuffs. He sat rock-still instead of jerking from side to side like Martineau. Then I noticed his ears."

"Roger, this is absolute nonsense. I now am going to bed and I hope to sleep. In the morning, if Mr. Martineau's ears still trouble you, you may confide your fears to Sir Henry, and perhaps he will be able to reassure you. Meanwhile I suggest that you get a good night's rest, as we leave promptly at nine o'clock in the morning."

The door closed; Roger slowly returned to the saloon. Here he sat and wrestled with his problem. Should he go to Sir Henry? Should he confront the counterfeit oboeist on his own responsibility? What a wretched situation! And Roger shook his head in dissatisfaction. There must be a simple manner in which to resolve the matter! For ten minutes he considered, then pounded the table softly with his fist. The solution leapt into mind!

The following morning final preparations were made for departure. At half-past eight one of the guards diffidently approached Dame Isabel. "Mr. Wool has not yet returned aboard, madame."

Dame Isabel looked blankly at the man. "Where in the world did he go?"

"He left the ship two hours ago; he stated that he had a message from you to deliver to the Governor."

"This is a most extraordinary situation! I certainly never sent him off with such a message! What could he be thinking of? I have a good mind to leave without him!"

Bernard Bickel approached, and Dame Isabel told him of Roger's eccentric conduct. "I fear his mind is going," said Dame Isabel. "Last night he came babbling of Mr. Martineau's ears; this morning he runs off with an imaginary message for the Governor!"

Bernard Bickel shook his head in perplexity. "I suppose we had better send the guard to look for him."

Dame Isabel compressed her lips. "This is an absolutely inexcusable irresponsibility! I am seriously of a mind to leave without him. He was well aware of my wish to leave at nine precisely."

"The only explanation can be that he has become temporarily deranged," said Bernard Bickel.

"Yes," muttered Dame Isabel. "I suppose you are right." She turned to the guard. "Mr. Wool must be found. Not inconceivably—on the supposition that he is indeed deranged—he went to the Governor's apartments bearing this imaginary message. I suggest that you seek there for him first."

But now at the entry-port there was altercation. Dame Isabel and Bernard Bickel, hastening to the port, found Roger and a disheveled Calvin Martineau arguing with the guard.

"You may come aboard, Mr. Wool. This other man may not, as the ship's roster is complete."

"I am Calvin Martineau," said the oboe-player in a weak but insistent voice. "I demand to be permitted aboard!"

"What is going on?" demanded Dame Isabel. "Mr. Martineau, what is the meaning of this peculiar situation?"

"I have been held prisoner!" cried Martineau. "Subjected to indignities. Drugged! Threatened! If it had not been for Mr. Wool I don't know what would have happened to me!"

"I told you that other oboeist was an impostor," said Roger.

Dame Isabel drew a deep breath. "And how did you know where to find Mr. Martineau?"

"It seemed simple enough. Faces can be changed, mannerisms can be faked—but only an oboe-player could successfully pass himself off for an oboe-player. So I knew that the false Martineau played the oboe, more than likely in the symphony. I learned where the Skylark Symphony oboeist lived, I went to the address, and walked in. Mr. Martineau was tied hand and foot under the bed."

Martineau broke into new complaints. Dame Isabel held up her hand. "Bernard, please take a guard into the ship and give the criminal into his custody."

Five minutes later the sullen impostor was marched off the ship. The resemblance to the authentic Calvin Martineau was remarkable. "How in the world—" began Bernard Bickel.

The Senior Inspector, who had been summoned, shook his head sadly. "Apparently there has been sly work at the Reconstruction Laboratories; I am amazed . . . And yet not too amazed. Many convicts would risk all their privileges for the chance to escape Skylark."

"I don't understand this at all," said Bernard Bickel. "How can one man's face be transferred to another?"

"I know little of the exact process," said the inspector, "but in the Reconstruction Laboratories these operations are not unknown. I believe a mold is made of the face to be duplicated. Then the second face is made pliable by various injections and forced into the mask. Providing the bone structure is not too obtrusively different, the flesh takes a temporary set into the features of the mold. Naturally the impostor and the victim must be of approximately similar physical structure for the simulation to be convincing."

"Remarkable!" said Bernard Bickel. "Well, well, Mr. Martineau, you are very lucky indeed." He turned back to the inspector. "You used the word 'temporary.' How long would the molded flesh retain its shape?"

"I don't know with any certainty. Perhaps a week or so."

Bernard Bickel nodded. "And then—who knows? The impostor might feign some sort of skin trouble and wrap up his face, or grow a beard. If we reached another port he could leave the ship."

"Diabolical!" muttered Dame Isabel. "Well, then. It is almost nine; we had better seal the ship. Roger, please stop fidgeting and come aboard, unless you wish to be left behind!"

"Just a minute!" cried Roger. "You can't leave now!"

"Any why not?"

"Don't you think we'd better check the rest of the

ship's company? There's no telling how many of these impostors are aboard."

Dame Isabel looked at him blankly, then said, "Ridiculous!" in a subdued voice.

Bernard Bickel said, "Do you know, I think he's absolutely right? We'll have to check the entire personnel of the ship."

Dame Isabel summoned Sir Henry Rixon, Andrei Szinc, Captain Gondar, and explained the circumstances. Captain Gondar said in a surly voice, "You can cross the crew off your list of suspects. None of us have left the ship, and you can check it by quartermaster records."

The records corroborated Captain Gondar's statement. Madoc Roswyn likewise had not set foot on the soil of Skylark.

Ada Francini, the excitable soprano, declared, "You think I am somebody else? You are crazy. Listen!" She sang an exercise, trilling up and down octaves as if they were thirds. "Can anyone sing like that but Francini?"

There was no contradiction. "Also," said Ada Francini, "I know the voice of every singer aboard the ship, and I know all the little secrets. Give me three minutes, I will show you the convicts."

While Ada Francini investigated the singers, listening to a scale or an exercise, asking whispered questions and hearing whispered answers, the Governor arrived, and was informed as to the state of affairs. He was shocked and distressed, and offered his most profound apologies to Dame Isabel.

Meanwhile Roger had taken Bernard Bickel to the side. "I'm obviously genuine, because I broke the whole thing wide open. Where did my aunt hire you?"

"In the rose garden at Ballew."

"Very good; you're genuine. I talked to Martineau. He's been kidnaped two days. That means for two days the other man was playing the oboe in the orchestra."

Bernard Bickel chewed his mustache. "The strings wouldn't pay any great attention, nor the brass. But the woodwinds—"

Roger nodded. "Exactly my thought. The woodwinds must all be bogus."

"I'll just have a word with Sir Henry—"

"No!" hissed Roger. "If the entire woodwind section is false, how could Sir Henry not be aware of it?"

"You mean—Sir Henry?"

"Obviously."

Bernard Bickel looked toward the group by the entrance-ramp. "You're right! Sir Henry is taller; furthermore he would never wear black shoes with a brown suit!"

The false Sir Henry heard his name. Furtively he looked around, and seeing that he was under suspicion tried to run off, but was caught and subdued.

"This is a disgraceful act!" exclaimed the Governor. "Do you realize it's transporation if the real Henry is harmed?"

The imposter gave a sickly grin. "No fear of that. I may be a failure, but I'm no fool." He gave directions as to where Sir Henry could be found; before long the enraged conductor was returned to the ship.

The state of affairs was explained to him, and he nodded balefully. "False musicians in the orchestra won't fool me, not for an instant. Everyone! Your instruments!"

The harpist, pianist and percussionist were allowed to prove their authenticity verbally, which they did after a set of quiet questions from Sir Henry.

The other musicians had tuned and were prepared. One after another Sir Henry examined them; one after another played brief passages and scales.

As Roger had anticipated, the woodwinds were all imposters. Threatened with transportation, they gave information as to where the missing musicians could be found and were marched away in the custody of guards.

Dame Isabel had watched the proceedings in growing consternation. "I still can't feel secure," she quavered. "Suppose we have missed someone? Isn't there some definite way to set my mind at peace?"

"We've checked everybody aboard," said Bernard Bickel. "All are safe and sound and accounted for. I suppose there's no reason why we can't take departure. Eh, Governor? Any objections?"

The Governor, who had been talking quietly to Roger, turned around. "What's this, sir?"

Bernard Bickel repeated his request.

"You want to leave, do you?" said the Governor. "Well, we'll have to discuss that. Ma'am, are you quite well?" He walked over to Dame Isabel, peered into her face. Then clamping a heavy hand on her neck, he shook her like a terrier shaking a rat. Off flew a wig, revealing a scalp covered with roached red hair. "You villain! Where is Dame Isabel? Do you realize that it's transportation if the slightest harm has been done?"

"No fear, the old crock's in good shape," said the simulated Dame Isabel, allowing his voice to resume its natural pitch.

Half an hour later the real Dame Isabel was brought back to the ship.

"This is a complete and absolute outrage!" she told the Governor. "Do you realize that for two days I've been penned up in a filthy den? At the mercy of rogues?"

"I confess my shame!" declared the Governor. "I am mortified beyond all account! You realize of course that you've got your nephew to thank for your safety. I can't imagine how he saw through the deception. How could you be so sure?" he asked Roger. "The impersonation seemed absolutely faultless!"

Roger glanced sidewise at Dame Isabel. "Well—there were small mistakes. The impostor seemed rather too placid, too mild. She only said 'Tut Tut,' or words to that effect to find that Sir Henry and the woodwinds were false. Aunt Isabel would have called out for boiling oil, or transportation at the very least. It seems a small thing, but it aroused my suspicions."

Dame Isabel marched furiously aboard the ship. "We depart at once," she rasped over her shoulder.

Bernard Bickel smiled wanly. "One thing I don't understand. If in a week the disguise would wear off—"

"They planned to take over the ship," said the Chief Inspector. "I've had a quiet chat with a clarinetist. Thanks to Mr. Wool, the plot failed."

Chapter Ten

FOR SEVERAL days a state of distrust persisted aboard the *Phoebus*, but finally all aboard were reassured. Dame Isabel remained in her cabin for some little time, emerging only at the news that Captain Gondar had gone mad.

The message, conveyed to Dame Isabel by the near-hysterical Hermilda Warn, was not completely accurate. Captain Gondar had not gone mad; he had merely tried to kill Logan de Appling with his bare hands. The Chief Technician and Bernard Bickel had intervened; struggling and kicking, Captain Gondar had been thrust into his cabin and there confined.

Dame Isabel hurried to the bridge, and finding it deserted, descended to the saloon, which was full of excited discussion. Gradually she pieced out the circumstances: apparently Captain Gondar had come upon Logan de Appling in the act of embracing Madoc Roswyn, and this triggered the explosion.

Dame Isabel heard the various versions of the affair silently, with no sign other than an ominous tightening of the lips. "And where is the young woman now?"

Madoc Roswyn had sought the seclusion of her cubicle. Ramona Thoxted and Cassandra Prouty, chancing to pass the door, reported hearing no sound from within. "If I had caused as much trouble and distress," declared Ramona Thoxted, "I would be utterly heartbroken. But I heard not a sound!"

Roger offered an explanation. "You probably did not have your ear pressed tightly enough against the door."

"That will do, Roger," said Dame Isabel sharply.

Bernard Bickel returned from the infirmary and Dame Isabel took him aside for consultation. Bickel's report of the episode generally tallied with that which Dame Isabel had already heard. "I simply don't know what to do!" she said in vexation. "I expected difficulties and misunderstandings, but it certainly seems that we are having more than our share. A good proportion of them can be traced to the Roswyn girl. I should have put her off at Sirius Planet!"

"Some people do seem to catalyze trouble," Bernard Bickel agreed. "But whatever the cause, the result is that we find ourselves temporarily without a captain."

Dame Isabel made an impatient gesture. "No great matter; Mr. de Appling can lay out our course and Mr. Henderson is entirely capable of performing Captain Gondar's other duties. I am mainly concerned about Rlaru. If Captain Gondar is too distrait or deranged or defiant to guide us there, we'll be seriously inconvenienced."

Bernard Bickel reflected. "In my opinion, we should allow the dust to settle. When Captain Gondar cools down, he'll come to his wits—after all it's to his advantage to guide us to Rlaru. Meanwhile young de Appling can take us to the next halt on our itinerary, which as I recall is the planet known as Swannick's Star."

"Yes. A wretched dirty little world reverted to feudalism."

Bernard Bickel raised his eyebrows. "I've always understood it to be a charming world, old-fashioned and quaint."

Dame Isabel gave a shaky laugh. "It well may be, Bernard. I'm in such a terrible mood that the Garden of Eden would seem a pest-hole . . . For all our undeniable successes, I am just a trifle discouraged."

Bernard Bickel gave a hearty laugh. "Come, that's no way to talk! Think of the reception we received at Skylark!"

Dame Isabel closed her eyes. "Never mention that planet! When I recall the utterly rude treatment I was accorded: the curses, the jeers, the coarse jokes . . . But I will not dwell on the episode. Success yes—of a sort. Remember, however, that these were Earthmen, starved for music, and it does not represent the kind of success I had hoped for. And Swannick's Star is basically more of the same."

"Eventually we will reach Rlaru," Bernard Bickel told her.

"I realize this—but are there no other cultured races in the universe?"

Bernard Bickel shrugged. "Frankly, I don't know of any."

"I suppose we must maintain our itinerary," said Dame Isabel resignedly. "There's Mr. de Appling; will you please call him over?"

Bernard Bickel summoned Logan de Appling. Dame Isabel surveyed him coldly. "I see you are not seriously hurt."

"I seem to have escaped with my life." And de Appling gave a shaky laugh. He was a tall blond young man, with an easy confident manner; there was no mystery as to why Madoc Roswyn might have preferred him to Captain Gondar.

"The next stop on our itinerary is Swannick's Star," said Dame Isabel. "I forget the formal description of the planet, but no doubt you have access to the appropriate references."

"Oh yes; quite so."

For Dame Isabel's taste Logan de Appling was somewhat too breezy. "Captain Gondar has decided to keep to his cabin for a few days," she said in her most formal voice. "You will therefore be responsible for astrogation."

Logan de Appling made one of his easy confident gestures. "No problem there; I'll take you to the Great Nebula if you like. Did you say Swannick's Star?"

"I did."

"Would you allow me to make a suggestion?"

"Certainly."

"Not far distant is a world which has been visited by

men no more than once or twice. As I understand it, this planet is superbly beautiful, inhabited by near-human creatures of advanced culture."

Bernard Bickel asked, "This world is in Hydra?"

Logan de Appling looked startled. "As a matter of fact, it is."

"And where did you hear of this world?" demanded Dame Isabel.

"From several sources." Logan de Appling fidgeted. "They all agree that—"

Dame Isabel pursued the subject relentlessly. "Would you be good enough to enlarge upon the nature of these sources?"

Logan de Appling scratched his head. "Let me think ... I believe that one of my astrogation manuals—"

"Let me ask you this: has Miss Roswyn mentioned this planet to you?"

Logan de Appling flushed. "Well, yes. As a matter of fact, she had heard something about it. We agreed that I should mention the planet to you."

"In short," said Dame Isabel in the iciest of voices, "she insisted that you recommend a visit to this planet."

"Well—I wouldn't say insisted."

"You may tell Miss Roswyn that under no circumstances will we cross half the galaxy in order to gratify her whims. We absolutely will not visit this world. Please do not mention it again."

Logan de Appling's face burned an angry red. "Just as you wish."

"Now, if you will, please verify that our present course is that which takes us most expeditiously to Swannick's Star."

Logan de Appling bowed, stalked away.

* * * * * *

Several days passed and still Captain Gondar did not show himself. "Let him stew in his own juice," Bernard Bickel advised. "The longer he sits the more amenable he'll be to reason."

Dame Isabel dubiously agreed. "A strange man indeed. But we cannot waste time analyzing his conduct . . . Do you suppose, Bernard, that our audience on Swannick's Star will consist entirely of the upper classes? If so, I might be inclined to another performance of *Fidelio*—or do you think we should undertake Wagner?"

"Either should be eminently suitable," said Bernard Bickel. "Still, we might at least consider Puccini . . ." He paused as Logan de Appling entered the saloon. Dame Isabel signaled: the young astrogator—rather reluctantly, or, so it seemed—approached. "How long before we reach Swannick's Star, Mr. de Appling?" asked Dame Isabel. "This seems a simply interminable journey, and I observe no star on the cross-hairs."

"Quite true; there is a local ether-drift which must be taken into account . . . We'll probably be another several days . . ."

"My word!" said Bernard Bickel, "I had no idea Swannick's Star was all that far!"

"Relax, Mr. Bickel; enjoy the scenery!" Logan de Appling smiled down at Dame Isabel and left the saloon.

After three days Captain Gondar still had not appeared, and Dame Isabel finally made up her mind to confer with him. As she and Bernard Bickel crossed the bridge, Logan de Appling and Madoc Roswyn stood talking in great animation. At the sight of Dame Isabel they abruptly fell silent.

Dame Isabel went to the view-screen, where a view of the cosmos was projected by the dephasing system. She checked the cross-hairs, turned to Logan de Appling. "Swannick's Star is that greenish sun dead ahead?" she inquired.

"It can't be," said Bernard Bickel. "Swannick's Star is an orange dwarf!"

"True," said Logan de Appling cheerfully. "We're allowing for space-drift and also galactic rotation, which in this region is quite considerable."

"Surely we should be closer to our destination!" said

Dame Isabel. "Are you absolutely sure of your calculations, Mr. de Appling?"

"Of course! It wouldn't do to get lost this far from home!"

Dame Isabel gave her head a puzzled shake. Crossing the bridge she knocked at Captain Gondar's door. "Yes?" came a surly voice from within. "Who is it?"

"It is I," said Dame Isabel. "I want a word or two with you."

The door flung open; Captain Gondar looked out. He was gaunt, his eyes glowed, a straggly black beard covered his cheeks and chin. "Well?" he croaked. "What do you want?"

"I'd like you to check the astrogation," said Dame Isabel in a mild voice. "I don't altogether trust the judgment of Mr. de Appling. It seems that we should long ago have reached Swannick's Star."

With four long strides Captain Gondar was on the bridge. He took one look at the view-screen, gave a harsh laugh. He paused, then laughed again, until Dame Isabel wondered whether he was mad indeed. She glanced at de Appling, who stood stifflly to the side, his fair cheeks flushing. She turned back to Captain Gondar. "Why do you laugh?"

Gondar pointed. "See the cant of the Milky Way? And that star off there to the right? That's Alphard or I'm a baboon. All of which puts us in Hydra."

"There must be some dreadful mistake," stammered Dame Isabel. "Swannick's Star is in Taurus."

Once more Captain Gondar vented his harsh croak of a laugh. "No mistake." He pointed a long finger at Madoc Roswyn. "That's why we're in Hydra."

Dame Isabel was speechless. She stared from Madoc Roswyn to Logan de Appling and back to Captain Gondar. "Do you mean—can it be—"

"He's taken you on a joy-ride. Don't blame him too much. I don't believe a man alive can stand up to her. She's a dire Welsh witch. If I were you I'd throw her into space and let her swim."

Dame Isabel swung about. In a terrible voice she asked, "Is this true, Mr. de Appling?"

"Yes."

"Captain, turn the ship about. Then confine these two to their respective cabins."

Gondar said, "Don't lock up de Appling. He's just a jackanapes. Make him work. If he swerves a second of an arc I'll strangle him. But lock her up. Keep her from the sight of men, or she'll use her magic."

"Very well. Miss Roswyn, to your cabin. I can't imagine how to deal with you."

"Put me in a life-boat and let me go off by myself."

Dame Isabel stared. "Are you serious?"

"Yes."

"Naturally," said Dame Isabel, "I shall do nothing of the sort. It would be nothing less than murder. To your cabin, if you please."

Madoc Roswyn went slowly from the bridge.

"As for you," Dame Isabel said to Logan de Appling, "Captain Gondar will note this occurrence in the log. You will receive no pay, and I shall take every step to ensure that you never again secure employment as an astrogator."

Logan de Appling said nothing. The heavens swung across the view-screen as Captain Gondar swung the *Phoebus* about on its axis.

* * * * * * *

Four hours later Roger tapped at Madoc Roswyn's door. Slowly the door opened and she looked at him.

"May I come in?" Roger asked.

Without speaking she drew listlessly back.

Roger seated himself on the bunk. "Have you eaten?"

"I'm not hungry." She moved across the little cubicle, to lean against the wall.

"If I only knew why you've been doing all this," said Roger tentatively. "It's beyond my understanding. How could anyone be so beguiling, so faithless—unless she had some overpowering motive?"

Madoc Roswyn hardly seemed to hear. She said in a low voice. "Do you think your aunt will . . ." Then she sighed, made a helpless motion. "I know she won't."

"I realize that you only pretended to be fond of me," went on Roger, "to get aboard the ship . . . And the same with Captain Gondar and that ass de Appling . . ."

Madoc Roswyn nodded drearily. "Yes. I only pretended. I had no other way."

"But why? If only I could understand why I might not think so harshly of you."

Madoc Roswyn looked at him with a ghost of a smile. "Do you think harshly of me, Roger?"

He nodded. "Yes. It's humiliating to be used."

"All I can say, Roger, is that I'm sorry. Really I am. But I'd do it again," she added in a low voice, "if it would help . . . But it won't."

"No. Not now. Tell me why."

"No . . . I don't think so."

"Why not?"

"Because I'm secretive. I'm born of secretive people. All my life I've had secrets you'd never dream of."

"No doubt," said Roger sadly. "No doubt."

She sat down, rather diffidently, on the bunk beside him. Roger swayed, as if he were iron and she a magnet. With an effort he brought himself to his previous position. After a moment's thought, he asked: "This planet in Hydra is one of your secrets?"

"Yes."

"If the *Phoebus* visited this planet, it would no longer be secret."

Now it was Madoc Roswyn's turn to ponder. "This had never occurred to me. But you must remember my upbringing. I've been habituated to secrecy."

"Secrecy," said Roger, "is a miserable vice. I have no secrets whatever."

Madoc Roswyn smiled wanly. "You're indeed an admirable man, Roger. Very well. I'll tell you my secret. It's all mine now, because none are left to share it. And since we're not to visit Yan, no one would believe either you or me."

" 'Yan' is the name of this planet?"

"Yan . . ." She breathed the name with the most fervent reverence and affection. "It is my home behind the stars. So near now, and so far."

Roger frowned in puzzlement. "Is this Welsh folk-lore? I'm sorry to be ignorant, but I've never heard anything like it before."

She shook her head. "I am not Welsh. Or not altogether Welsh. Long long ago—thirty thousand years . . ." She talked for an hour, and Roger's head swam with the marvels which came casually from her lips.

Shorn of detail and circumstance her story was simple enough. Thirty thousand years ago a race of Earth-folk inhabited a pleasant land whose exact location was now unknown—some thought it to be Greenland, others the land now submerged below the Bay of Biscay. They attained civilization, of a texture as rich as any of those which followed. During a period of decadence, a certain arcane group contrived a ship of space and exiled themselves from Earth. After an epic voyage they landed on Yan, which they made their home. And what of the once-noble civilization which had been left behind? Its destiny no one ever learned: apparently it spent itself and lapsed to ruins.

On Yan a new era began, with advances, retreats, dark ages, renewals, culminations, aftermaths. Then, two hundred years ago, another dissident group decided to return to Earth. Their landing on the Isle of Man was a catastrophe which destroyed the ship and all but a handful of the passengers. These fled the superstitious persecution of the Manxmen and settled in Wales, where for generations they farmed the remote valleys of Merioneth. Such were Madoc Roswyn's forebears, who perpetuated their traditions, whispered the history of Yan to their children, dedicated themselves to secrecy. They lived only to return to Yan, and bred this yearning into their children. One of these was Madoc Roswyn, the last of her line. Longing for Yan, she had taken advantage of Roger's bemusement to win herself passage on the *Phoebus*.

She finished her story. She had tried and failed; Yan was now forever lost to her.

Roger sat quietly a long moment, then heaved a sigh. "I'll help you as best I can. If I succeed it means I've lost you forever—but not really, because I can't lose something I've never had . . . I'll talk to my aunt."

Madoc Roswyn said nothing, but when Roger departed, she slumped back on the bunk and tried to restrain the tears which welled from behind her eyelids.

* * * * * * *

Roger found Dame Isabel on the bridge, trying to learn the exact location of Rlaru from a brooding and taciturn Captain Gondar. His only reply to her expostulations was, "All in good time, all in good time."

Roger attracted Dame Isabel's attention and asked to speak with her in private. With poor grace she acceded, and took him to her cabin. Here walking back and forth he said, "I know you consider me a wastrel, and credit me with very little judgment."

"Do I not have reason to do so?" inquired Dame Isabel with acerbity. "You brought that dreadful young woman aboard the *Phoebus*. She has disrupted the entire tour!"

"Yes," said Roger. "Quite true. I've just learned the motive for her acts. It's a strange tale, and I'd like you to hear it."

"Roger, I am not all that ingenuous; nothing would be gained."

"She is not what you think," said Roger, "and her motive for wanting to visit this particular world is astonishing."

"I do not wish to be astonished," growled Dame Isabel. "I have had enough surprises . . . I suppose, in simple justice, I must speak to this wretched girl. Where is she?"

"In her cabin. I'll fetch her."

Madoc Roswyn was extremely reluctant to talk to Dame Isabel. "She hates me. She senses things in me she can't understand, that she doesn't want to understand. She'd listen to me only to find exercise for her sarcasm."

"Come now," said Roger. "Isn't it worth a try? What can you lose? Just tell her what you told me. How can she help but be impressed?"

"Very well," said Madoc Roswyn. "I'll do it . . . Let me wash my face."

Roger took Madoc Roswyn to Dame Isabel's cabin and prudently retired to the corridor. For an hour he heard the soft lilt of Madoc Roswyn's voice, with occasionally a crisp question or remark from Dame Isabel. At last he deemed it judicious to enter; and neither Dame Isabel nor Madoc Roswyn seemed to notice his presence.

Madoc Roswyn finally completed her story, and Dame Isabel sat silent, drumming her fingers on the arm of her chair. "What you tell me is extremely interesting," she said at last. "I cannot deny it. While I will never condone your acts, I admit that you have put forward a compelling motive—provided it can be sustained. Interesting indeed . . ." She gave Roger a sour smile. "Well—stubborn inflexibility is a fault of which I have never been accused." She turned back to Madoc Roswyn. "Tell me something more of the planet, of its customs and institutions."

Madoc Roswyn shook her head uncertainly. "I wouldn't know where to begin. Earth history is six thousand years old, the history of Yan is five times longer."

"Let me ask this: do your traditions mention art and music?"

"Oh yes, indeed." Madoc Roswyn sang an odd little song in a strange language. The melody, the rhythm, the meter of the language derived from human perceptions and human needs—so much was intuitively clear—but also conveyed a quality which had no terrestrial reference: in short, the music of another planet. "That's a nursery song," said Madoc Roswyn. "From as early as I can remember, and before, I went to sleep by that song."

Dame Isabel signaled Roger. "Please ask Captain Gondar to step in here a moment, if he'll be so good."

Captain Gondar appeared.

Dame Isabel said in a clear cool voice, "I have decided to convey Miss Roswyn to the planet Yan. She has worked with great diligence to this end, by expedients I will not comment upon. I am not completely convinced that I have heard the precise and entire truth, but Miss Roswyn has intrigued me to the extent that I wish to learn the facts. So, Captain—set a new course, to Yan, as I believe the planet is known."

Captain Gondar gave Madoc Roswyn a black look. "She's scheming and faithless; she knows every evil to be learned in the far Welsh mountains; you'll regret the day she persuaded you."

"Quite possibly," said Dame Isabel. "Nevertheless, to Yan."

Madoc Roswyn waited silently until Captain Gondar had departed. Then she turned to Dame Isabel. "Thank you," she said, and left the cabin.

Chapter Eleven

ON THE cross-hairs once more lay that greenish-white
sun described in the Star Directory as Hydra GRA 4442.
The tale told by Madoc Roswyn had circulated throughout the *Phoebus,* predictably encountering incredulity.
The general consensus was that, whether or not the *Phoebus* would find an age-old civilization on Yan, the upshot
was certain to be dramatic, and the atmosphere was taut
with expectancy.

The green star flared large and moved to the side: in
the cross-hairs hung an Earth-sized planet, well within the
zone of habitability. The *Phoebus* slipped out of star-
drive, swung into a normal approach orbit.

On the bridge Dame Isabel, Captain Gondar, Madoc
Roswyn and Roger stood looking into the view-screen as
Yan rolled magnificently below. No question but what it
was a beautiful planet, not dissimilar from Earth. There
were oceans and continents, mountains and deserts,
forests and tundras and ice-fields, and the analyzer indicated a breathable atmosphere.

Captain Gondar said in a carefully expressionless voice,
"No response to our radio signal—in fact we can't inter-
cept signals on any wave-length whatever."

"Odd," said Dame Isabel. "Let us examine the surface
more closely. Can you increase the magnification on the
screen?"

Captain Gondar adjusted the view-screen, the surface
seemed to leap closer.

Madoc Roswyn pointed. "I recognize those continents.
That's Esterlop and Kerlop, and there in the north is

Noauluth. That big island is Drist Amiamu, those little ones are the Suthore Stil. That long peninsula is Drothante, and there are six great temples at the extreme southern cape." She looked carefully into the magnified image, but the tip of the long peninsula showed no sign of the temples she had mentioned. "I don't understand," she muttered in a low voice. "Nothing looks as it should . . . Where is Dilicet? Thax? Koshiun?"

"I see no obvious signs of habitation," said Dame Isabel drily.

"There are ruins," Roger pointed out. "Or rough patches which look like ruins."

"Down there, beside that bay, where the forest runs up over the mountain—that is where I expected to find Sansue, the city of my ancestors. But where? More ruins?"

"If ruins, they are certainly thorough-going ruins," said Roger. "Not one stone seems to be left on another."

"From this height, through so much air and mist, details are deceptive," said Captain Gondar grudgingly. "I don't believe you could distinguish a city from ruins."

"I see no reason why we should not land," said Dame Isabel, "using all due caution, of course."

The *Phoebus* swooped down into its landing spiral, and presently details of the surface revealed themselves. Cities there were none, only tumbles of broken stone, vast areas of scorch and char and rubble. Dame Isabel said to Madoc Roswyn. "You are sure this is the correct planet?"

"Yes, of course! Something terrible has happened!"

"Well, we shall soon find out. That area beside the bay is your ancestral home?"

Madoc Roswyn gave an uncertain affirmative; Dame Isabel nodded to Captain Gondar, the *Phoebus* settled a mile to the east of the city Sansue, on a stretch of stony ground, less than a hundred yards from the edge of a dense forest.

The almost insensible vibration of the various engines died to quietness. The analyzers indicated a salubrious atmosphere; the exit-port opened; the ramp touched the soil of Yan.

Captain Gondar, Dame Isabel, Madoc Roswyn came slowly forth, followed by Bernard Bickel, Roger and the rest of the company. For half an hour they stood breathing the strangely scented air of Yan, while the green-white sun sank below the horizon.

The quiet was profound, broken only by the quiet voices of the folk from the *Phoebus*. Madoc Roswyn wandered up a little rise and stood looking west into the twilight. Here and there rose hummocks overgrown with grass and shrubbery; they might have been ruins but details were blurred in the dusk. The faint wind which blew over the plain carried a peculiar musty odor, perhaps deriving from the vegetation or the shore, or perhaps from the hummocks themselves.

Madoc Roswyn started to move forward, as if to go down into the plain, but Roger, who had come quietly behind her, took her arm. "Not in the dark. It might be dangerous."

"I don't understand any of this," she said in an anguished mutter. "What has happened to Yan?"

"Perhaps the traditions of your people were incorrect."

"It can't be! All my life I have planned to visit this city—I know it as well as you know any city of Earth. I know the avenues, the plazas, the halls; I could find the quarter where my ancestors lived before they departed, perhaps the very palace . . . Now there is nothing but ruins."

Roger gently drew her toward the ship. "It's getting dark."

She came reluctantly. "I'm hated by everyone aboard the ship . . . They think terrible things of me—and now they think me a fool as well."

"Of course not," said Roger soothingly. "At the worst you made an honest mistake."

Madoc Roswyn held up her hand. "Listen!" From the forest came a low-pitched ululation, which might have been produced by a human throat. It carried a whole complex of overtones, and produced an indefinable sensation in Roger. He tugged at Madoc Roswyn's arm more urgently. "Let's get back to the ship."

She came with him; they circled the ship to the entrance-ramp, where a group stood looking toward the forest, taut with the half-pleasurable dread of the unknown. Again came the low-pitched wail, perhaps a trifle closer.

The twilight was now almost gone; only a dim olive-green glow remained in the west. The ship's floodlights came on, illuminating the area around the ship and bathing the little group in brightness. There was a sound from the forest, a whisper of disturbed air, and a stone struck the ground only five feet from Roger.

Everyone shrank back against the hull, then hastened up the ramp into the ship.

In the morning Dame Isabel discussed the situation with Madoc Roswyn, Bernard Bickel and Roger. She had not slept well, and spoke very tartly. "Circumstances are not as I had expected, and I confess that I'm at a loss as how to proceed." And she glanced around the group.

"I suppose we could send out the lifeboat to reconnoiter the planet," Bernard Bickel put forward thoughtfully.

"To what purpose?" inquired Dame Isabel. "We saw no cities, nor even centers of primitive civilization from the reconnaissance orbit."

"True."

Dame Isabel turned to Madoc Roswyn. "You are certain that this is the correct planet?"

"Yes."

"Strange."

"There seem to be a great number of ruins," suggested Roger. "It might be—" his voice trailed off.

"Might be what, Roger?" inquired his aunt in her most acid tones.

"I'm not sure."

"Your remark then is superfluous. Please don't dither; we have more than enough distraction as it is. While I do not necessarily doubt Miss Roswyn's word, the possibility remains that she is mistaken. In any case, the net result is the same: we have been brought far out of the way on a wild goose chase."

Madoc Roswyn rose to her feet, departed the room. Roger scowled at Dame Isabel. "There obviously has been a civilization here, of some sort, at some time."

"We can only hypothesize as much. One thing you must learn, Roger, is that idle philosophizing will never put bread and butter in your mouth."

Bernard Bickel tactfully intervened. "As Roger points out, there seem to be ruins about—and beyond dispute there is sentient life in the forest. Personally, I'm quite willing to believe that Miss Roswyn brought us here in good faith."

"Miss Roswyn's good faith or lack of it are not the immediate question," snapped Dame Isabel. "What concerns me—"

The mess steward appeared in the doorway. "Miss Roswyn has left the ship," he blurted. "She's gone into the forest!"

Roger sprang from the saloon, ran pell-mell along the corridor down the off-ramp. Here he found a group of musicians who had been sunning themselves but who now stood gazing uneasily toward the forest.

"What happened?" asked Roger.

"The girl went crazy!" a cellist told him. "She came out of the ship, stood looking at the forest, then before we could stop her, she just ran off—through there." He pointed. Roger went a few tentative steps toward the forest, peered into the dim shadows. The trees were similar to those of Earth, somewhat thicker of trunk, with a black-brown bark and foliage of various tones of green, green-blue, dark blue. Below, in the mulch of dead leaves, were marks of Madoc Roswyn's passage.

Roger edged toward the forest, trying to see through the shadows. And now there came a sudden sharp scream muffled by distance. Roger hesitated the time between heart-beats, then plunged into the forest.

Abruptly he was in a new world. Foliage cut off the

sunlight, dead leaves were soft underfoot, and gave off a resinous rank odor as he disturbed them. There were no sounds in the forest: it was as quiet as a closed room, and there were no signs of small life: birds, insects, rodents and the like.

Roger went on a space in a mingling of urgency and awe, until the traces left by Madoc Roswyn became confused. He halted, suddenly feeling helpless and futile. He went forward a few paces, called. There was no reply: his voice lost itself among the tree trunks.

He cleared his throat, called again, more loudly . . . He felt a prickling at the back of his neck, and turned about, but saw nothing. He stole forward, twenty feet, fifty feet, dodging from tree trunk to tree trunk, then paused to listen. From somewhere came a rustle of leaves, and a stone thudded against the tree trunk six inches from his head. He stared down at it as if mesmerized: it was round and black, about three inches in diameter. He swung about, crouching; another smaller stone struck him in the side. Two more stones hissed by his head, another bruised his leg. Roger roared out curses and insults, ingloriously retreated . . . The edge of the forest was farther than he remembered; he felt a wave of panic: was he lost? Ahead came the gleam of light and a moment later he came blinking out into the open a hundred yards from where he had entered. There was the *Phoebus*. Ungainly construction of globes and tubes though it might be, it seemed the most secure, desirable shelter imaginable. He hurried across the open space, limping on his bruised leg and holding his aching ribs.

Almost all the company stood in front of the ship, Captain Gondar, Neil Henderson and Bernard Bickel with hand-weapons. Dame Isabel cried out sharply, "Roger, what in the world possessed you to act like that?"

"I went to help Miss Roswyn," said Roger. He looked hopelessly toward the forest. "I heard her scream. I thought I could help her."

"The impulse was rash and foolish," said Dame Isabel

severely. Then she added in a kinder voice: "Though by no means discreditable."

"If we unshipped the lifeboat," said Roger desperately, "and flew over the forest—"

"It would be useless," said Bernard Bickel. "To do any good we'd be forced to fly at tree-top level, and who knows what capabilities the creatures have? A well-aimed arrow could disable the boat."

"I don't want to seem unkind," said Dame Isabel, "but I refuse to let anyone risk their life to no purpose."

Captain Gondar muttered, "She's probably dead right now."

And all again fell silent, looking off toward the forest.

"I frankly don't know what to do," said Dame Isabel finally. "There seems no possibility of making contact with the creatures who inhabit this world. And no matter how much we regret this terrible occurrence we can't remain here indefinitely."

"We can't just abandon her!" protested Roger in a shocked voice.

"I'm willing to make any reasonable effort on her behalf," said Dame Isabel, "but we can't overlook the fact that she went off of her own volition, without taking the slightest counsel of myself or Mr. Bickel or Captain Gondar. She is, or was, a very disturbed and erratic young woman; I don't feel that we are justified in taking drastic risks or allowing the basic purpose of the expedition to be perverted by this young woman's self-centered ambitions."

Roger could produce no convincing rejoinder. He looked to Bernard Bickel and Captain Gondar for support, but found none.

"We just can't go away and leave her!" he repeated desperately.

Bernard Bickel said in a gloomy voice, "there's not much else we can do."

Roger turned to look at the forest. "All the rest of my life," he said, "I'd wonder what had happened to her. Whether she were still alive, waiting for someone to come for her. Just imagine yourself out there, hurt, or perhaps tied to a tree, seeing the *Phoebus* rise up into the sky and leave."

There was silence. Then Bernard Bickel said with sub-dued intensity: "If we could only establish contact! If there were some way to demonstrate that we were not an-tagonistic!"

"According to Madoc Roswyn," said Roger, "the people were music lovers—why don't we put on a per-formance where they can see it? If anything would con-vince them of our good intentions, that should do it."

Bernard Bickel turned to Dame Isabel. "Why not?"

"Very well," said Dame Isabel. "Necessarily we will be forced to play here, in front of the ship. The acoustics will be vile. Still, the scheme is worth trying. Captain, will you have the piano brought out? Andrei, look to the sets; not the backdrops, but a few symbolical properties."

"Of course. And the opera?"

"I think--yes, I feel that *Pelleas and Melisande* will be as happy a choice as any."

* * * * * * *

The green-seeming sun approached the horizon; the sets were ready; a dais for the orchestra had been ar-ranged; a sound amplification system was directed toward the forest.

The musicians and singers ate a rather tense dinner, conversing in low voices: the performance they were about to put on, to an unseen and unknown audience, would be perhaps the most taxing of their lives.

In the green-gray dusk the musicians went to their in-struments. The air was even more still than on the previ-ous evening: from the forest came not the slightest whisper of sound. The instruments were tuned; small lights illumined the music stands. A pink spot played on Sir Henry Rixon; tall, handsome, impeccably dressed, he made a grave bow toward the forest, raised his baton. The music of Debussy flowed across the night and into the forest.

Spotlights illuminated the first set: a mythical forest and a fountain. The opera proceeded, and the attention from the forest was almost palpable. The first act gave way to the second act, and now the music reached that rare and wonderful region where it seemed to move of itself, naturally and inexorably . . . There was motion at the edge of the forest. Into the reach of the light staggered Madoc Roswyn. She was bruised, haggard, dirty; her garments were torn, her eyes were bright; she moved with a strange jerking motion, like a walking doll with a broken mechanism. Roger ran forth to meet her; she almost fell into his arms. Bernard Bickel came to help; they took her back to the ship. All the while the music proceeded; the fated lovers moved to their destiny.

"What happened?" . . . Roger asked in anguish. "Are you harmed, or injured?"

She made a gesture which might have meant anything. "Evil is here," she said in a husky broken voice. "We must leave, and put Yan far out of our mind."

Dame Isabel said, "You must come inside, child; Dr. Shand will look after you. We will leave tomorrow morning—"

Madoc Roswyn laughed harshly. She gestured back to the forest. "They listen to the music; it is the first heard on Yan for hundreds of years. They listen but they hate you for it, and as soon as the music stops they will attack the ship."

"What's this?" demanded Dame Isabel. "Why would they do such a thing?"

"They listen," said Madoc Roswyn, "but they listen in envy, knowing themselves and what they have done to Yan . . ."

"This is ridiculous," Dame Isabel declared. "I can't credit human beings with such malevolence . . . They are human I presume?"

"It makes no difference," said Madoc Roswyn in a weary half-whisper. "They came to listen and to prepare their vengeance; they forgot me and I was able to slip through the forest toward the music." She turned toward the ship. "Please let me go aboard the ship; I want to be clear of this dreadful planet . . ."

Roger and Dr. Shand took her aboard the ship. Dame Isabel turned to Bernard Bickel. "What is your opinion, Bernard?"

"She knows more about these people than we do; I think we should be ready to leave as soon as the opera is over."

"And leave our sets behind? Never!"

"Then we had better start taking the sets aboard; we can do this inconspicuously and the music can continue as long as necessary. I'll go have a word with Andrei and Sir Henry."

The opera went into the fifth act; the crew carried the used sets back into the ship. The opera ended; the music continued. More of Debussy: the *Nocturnes*. The last of the sets were carried aboard, then the lighting system, and the sound-amplifiers.

The orchestra, who now understood the nature of the situation, played on, glancing nervously from the corners of their eyes toward the forest.

The chairs were taken from under them, and Sir Henry's podium: they played standing. Word was passed that all was secure: under cover of a constantly shifting spotlight, the musicians one by one took their music stands and instruments and slipped aboard the ship, with the harpist and the percussionist assisted by crew-members. Finally only Sir Henry, the great resonant piano and the violins remained outside; and now the folk in the forest comprehended what was afoot, and awoke from their dreaming. A rock arched down from space, struck the piano keyboard.

Bernard Bickel called, "All into the ship, everybody! Quick!"

The pianist, the violinists and Sir Henry ran for the ramp, and just barely escaped the rocks which struck down where they had been standing. Out in the shadows there was movement, a dark sliding forward. The ramp was pulled aboard, the port snapped shut; the *Phoebus* rose into the night, leaving behind the polished black grand piano.

Dame Isabel, more relieved than she would have admitted to anyone, marched into the infirmary, where Madoc Roswyn, in a white nightgown, lay quietly in a hospital bed. Her eyes were open, focused on a point somewhere beyond the ceiling. Dame Isabel looked questioningly at Dr. Shand, who nodded. "She'll be all right. Shock, exhaustion, bruises. She wants no sedation."

Dame Isabel approached the bed. "I am extremely sorry you suffered as you did—but you should never have run into the forest."

"I had to know the truth of Yan."

"You found out," said Dame Isabel drily.

"Yes."

"Exactly who is it that lives in the forest? What has happened to them?"

Madoc Roswyn seemed not to hear. She stared at the point beyond the ceiling for almost half a minute. Dame Isabel peevishly repeated her question.

Madoc Roswyn shook her head. "I do not care to say. It is no longer important. If I say one word, then I will never be free of the subject. No. I will say nothing. Henceforth I know nothing of the Yan that was. I am only Madoc Roswyn of Merioneth, and I will never again be anything more."

Dame Isabel left the infirmary, marched to the saloon where singers and musicians were drinking wine rather freely and comparing their impressions of the performance.

Dame Isabel took Bernard Bickel aside. "The girl will say absolutely nothing of what occurred in the forest, or what has happened to that wretched planet! I have never known anyone so completely self-centered! Surely she must know that we are all curious!"

Bernard Bickel nodded. "Perhaps she is right. Perhaps it is better that Yan remain a mystery."

"Bernard, you are an incorrigible romantic!"

"No less than yourself! If not, would we be here in the first place?"

Dame Isabel gave a sour laugh. "Of course you are right . . . Well, well, then: so ends our visit to Yan. And now there have been enough preliminaries, as many casual detours as necessary. We will take ourselves directly to Rlaru, with no further diversions or delays." She rose to her feet. "Perhaps you will come with me to the bridge, while I give Captain Gondar his orders."

Captain Gondar stood alone looking out into the great glittering expanse of the cosmos. The ship had not yet gone into space-drive and the view was the natural light of the stars.

"From here, Captain," said Dame Isabel, "we will set a course directly to Rlaru."

Captain Gondar drew a deep breath. "That's a terrible long pull. The detour into Hydra took us far off course. We can return to Earth almost as easily."

"No, Captain," said Dame Isabel inexorably. "I insist that we pursue our original plans. Rlaru will be the next stop."

Captain Gondar's chin sagged, the shadows under his eyes suddenly seemed darker. He turned away, looked out across space. "Very well," he said in a muffled voice, "I will take you to Rlaru."

Chapter Twelve

BACK ACROSS the galaxy fled the *Phoebus*; through the Orion Sector, where Rigel occulted a far dim star which was Home Sun. The mood of the opera company was subdued, but morale had not deteriorated. As two pianos had been included among the orchestra properties, rehearsals continued without interruption.

Madoc Roswyn remained in the infirmary three days. Dr. Shand reported to Dame Isabel that only youth and vitality had brought her back to the *Phoebus*; whoever or whatever had attacked her might well have left her for dead. Roger sat with her for long periods; at times a trace of her old self would show itself; at other times she seemed to be reliving the events in the forest, when she would wince and close her eyes and turn her face to the wall; but for the most part she lay quietly, watching Roger.

Logan de Appling stalked about his duties in silence and injured dignity. Captain Gondar had disassociated himself from everything but his own inner existence and except for a minimum participation in the business of the ship spoke to no one. Dame Isabel attempted to extract detailed information regarding Rlaru, but Captain Gondar seemed absent-minded and vague.

Dame Isabel inquired sharply: "The inhabitants are quite friendly?"

Captain Gondar turned his head, and his sunken eyes gradually came into focus. "Friendly? You saw the Ninth Company, did they seem unfriendly?"

"No, of course not. Although I have always considered

141

their abrupt departure rather ungracious, in view of our efforts."

Captain Gondar ventured no opinion of his own.

Dame Isabel returned to the subject of Rlaru itself. "I believe you stated that you had photographed the planet?"

Captain Gondar looked at her blankly. "Did I tell you that?"

"Yes, during our original negotiations."

"I don't recall the circumstances."

Dame Isabel said briskly, "I would now like to be shown these photographs. There can be no possible reason for further caution."

Grudgingly Captain Gondar went to his cabin, returning with a plain white envelope, from which he took three rumpled photographs.

Dame Isabel gave him a stern glance, as if in admonishment for unnecessary circumspection. She took the photographs and examined them. The lack of detail was disappointing. The first had been recorded from a height of perhaps 500 miles, the second from 100 miles, the last from about five miles. The first showed a wide ocean, a north continent with a long peninsula depending into the temperate zone. The second showed the southern end of the peninsula, and hinted of the relief: low mountains to the north, hills rolling south to a nearly flat river-plain at the southern cape. The third picture, somewhat blurred, showed a shore-line, a river meandering between wide terraces, a hint of what might have been cultivated fields.

Dame Isabel frowned. "These photographs are hardly informative. You have nothing depicting the people, their cities, their architecture, their rituals?"

"No. I did not take the camera from the ship."

Dame Isabel examined the third photograph once again. "I presume this represents the area where you landed?"

Captain Gondar looked at the photograph as if he hardly recognized it. "Yes," he said at last. "This is where I landed—here." He touched a spot with his finger.

"The inhabitants gave you a hospitable greeting?"

"Oh yes. No difficulty of any sort."

Dame Isabel surveyed him keenly. "You sound just a trifle uncertain."

"Not at all. Although 'hospitable' isn't quite the right word. They accepted me without much interest of any kind."

"Hmm. Weren't they surprised to see you?"

"Difficult to say. They showed no great interest in me."

"Did they show curiosity in regard to Earth, or your spaceship?"

"No, not to any great extent."

"Hmmf. One would think them a stolid or stupidly introverted people, were it not for the evidence of the Ninth Company to the contrary . . ." Dame Isabel questioned Captain Gondar further, but received little added information.

Days went by, each with some small event to set it apart from every other. Madoc Roswyn left the infirmary, and retreated into herself even more completely than before. The singers and musicians indulged in occasional spasms of temperament; the Tough Luck Jug Band, disregarding Dame Isabel's interdict, produced what Ephraim Zerner described as "mind-shattering cacophony." Bernard Bickel, once more dispatched to quell the disturbance, was threatened with physical harm by the washboard player, whom he subsequently described as "intoxicated and truculent." Neil Henderson, the Chief Technician, intervened before the threat was put into effect, and Bernard Bickel returned to the saloon, furious at the insolence he had encountered.

More days went by. The *Phoebus*, entering Cetus, passed close by the star Xi Arietis, the seventh planet of which supported a Starline Freight terminus. During one of his moody perambulations Roger Wool chanced to walk by the pod in which the lifeboat was housed. By sheer chance he noticed the port swinging shut, a situation contrary to ship's regulations, which required that access to the lifeboat be at all times free and unconstricted. Hurrying forward Roger caught the port, just before it closed. He jerked it open and in doing so, brought Captain Gondar stumbling back out into the corridor.

Captain Gondar's expression of startled anger changed comically to affability. "Just checking up on lifeboat equipment," he said. "Part of my weekly routine."

Roger made a skeptical sound. "Why close the port?"

Captain Gondar's expression changed again to sternness. "What affair is it of yours how I order my work?"

Roger shrugged. He went to the lifeboat port, peered inside, to be seized by the shoulder and flung back into the corridor—but not before he had seen a suitcase and a duffel bag. Captain Gondar's face was now congested with rage. He snatched for his pocket and pulled forth a small hand-weapon: Roger thought to see murder in Captain Gondar's face. He forced his paralyzed muscles to act: never had they felt so limp. He dodged, struck out, and more by accident than design struck the gun from Captain Gondar's hand. Gondar hissed, panted, bent for the gun; Roger gave him a violent shove, kicked the gun rattling down the corridor.

Gondar had now lost all control of his emotions. He hurled himself upon Roger; the two tumbled back and forth in the corridor, striking, kicking, shoving.

The noise attracted attention; Neil Henderson and a pair of crew-men were suddenly between the two men, thrusting them apart. "Just what's this all about?" demanded Henderson.

Captain Gondar raised a trembling hand, pointed to Roger. But words refused to come to his mouth, and his arm dropped.

Roger panted, "He was going to kill me . . . I stopped him from going off in the lifeboat . . ."

Captain Gondar had been sidling down the corridor. He lunged for the gun; again Roger dived at him, blocked him away. Henderson seized the gun. "Now then, this is a serious business! What are the facts of the matter?"

"In the lifeboat is his luggage," panted Roger. "He was

planning to desert the *Phoebus* and make for the Starline Terminal."

Captain Gondar, curling his lip, said nothing.

Henderson stepped into the lifeboat, and emerged with a grim expression. "Take that stuff out," he told one of the crewmen, and to Captain Gondar: "Come along; we'd better talk this over with the big-wigs."

Dame Isabel heard the news in ominous silence. When Roger finished his account, she turned the full force of her gaze upon Captain Gondar. "Do you have any answer to make?"

"No."

"You must realize that by your acts you have forfeited all claim to the money I hold in trust."

"Not at all," said Gondar in a disdainful voice. "I have fulfilled my commitments."

"You have not taken us to Rlaru. The precise location of the planet is still known only to you."

"Wrong," said Captain Gondar. "This morning I made a detailed memorandum and gave it to de Appling. You cannot take my money on that pretext."

"We'll see about that," said Dame Isabel. "It seems to me that while serving the letter of the agreement, you have done violence to the spirit."

"I think not," said Captain Gondar. "However, I do not care to argue the matter, as I am presently at a disadvantage."

"Indeed you are. I hardly know what to do with you. Obviously your authority is at an end."

Gondar had regained his poise; he bowed with ironic grace. "Since you refuse to allow me the lifeboat, I ask only that you put me off at the Starline Terminal at Xi Arietis Seven."

"I will do nothing of the sort. Xi Arietis is considerably out of the way, and we have already engaged in one time-consuming detour."

Adolph Gondar scowled, then shrugged. Obviously he had expected no more. "In that case, I ask only that I be relieved of responsibility for the running of the ship."

"There is no difficulty as to this," said Dame Isabel drily.

"Also I wish to be allowed to keep to my cabin, for such time as I see fit."

"For such time as I see fit," said Dame Isabel. "Your inclinations need not enter into the situation. Perhaps you'll tell me why you chose to act in this fashion?"

"Certainly," said Adolph Gondar courteously. "I suddenly became anxious to leave the ship."

Dame Isabel turned to Chief Technician Henderson and Bernard Bickel. "Please conduct Mr. Gondar to his cabin. Make certain that he has no further weapons. Mr. Henderson, you will see that a suitable lock is attached to the door."

Adolph Gondar strode from the room, followed by Henderson and Bernard Bickel.

* * * * * * *

The *Phoebus* fleeted across the intersteller void, possibly as fast as thought, the velocity of which was yet a moot point. Logan de Appling indeed had been entrusted with Rlaru's coordinates: the sun was that yellow-orange star Cetus FQR910, which at last appeared on the crosshairs. In due course a single planet could be distinguished. The *Phoebus* slid in close, went into reconnaissance orbit. Any planet observed from space is an awesome sight, its massive sphericity emphasized by the harsh contrast of sunlit surface against the black of the void. If the planet appears to be habitable and displays an interesting configuration, then the provocation to the imagination is almost intolerable.

Rlaru was just such a world, in size and general aspect not unlike Earth: perhaps a trifle smaller and certainly of a more mature physiography. The environment analyzers reported conditions benign to human existence, with temperatures at poles and equator roughly equivalent to those of Earth.

In awe and exultation Dame Isabel and Bernard Bickel stood gazing at the slow-spinning globe. "Think, Bernard!" she exclaimed. "After all these months of planning and preparation! Rlaru at last! The home of the Ninth Company!"

"A beautiful world, to be sure," Bernard Bickel agreed.

"And look!" Dame Isabel took his arm, pointed. "There is the peninsula of Mr. Gondar's photographs! It's proof—if we needed any—that this is indeed Rlaru!"

"I wish I could understand Gondar's actions," said Bickel. "When you consider them carefully, they seem—almost sinister."

"Surely you're joking?"

"Not altogether."

Dame Isabel shook her head dubiously. "Mr. Gondar has assured me time and time again that the inhabitants are friendly. I have no reason to suspect otherwise; indeed, the Ninth Company seemed gracious enough—though I must say Mr. Gondar kept them in seclusion."

"There's no use borrowing trouble." Bernard Bickel returned to an inspection of the planet. "Where do you propose to put down?"

"At Mr. Gondar's original landing. We know that the folk are friendly here, whereas conditions elsewhere might be otherwise."

She gave the necessary instructions to Logan de Appling, who made appropriate adjustments at the automatic pilot. Rlaru bulked and bulged, and suddenly underwent that peculiar psychological ninety-degree shift in position, jumping from "across" to "below."

Logan de Appling radioed down for permission to land, using interstellar signal code, but received no acknowledgment. He looked questioningly toward Dame Isabel. "We will land," she said.

Using the macro-viewer Dame Isabel and Bernard Bickel carefully studied the face of Rlaru. They could find no evidence of an advanced civilization. Bernard Bickel pointed out a massive tumulus, and suggested that it might represent ruins; to which Dame Isabel made no response, the incident at the planet Yan being too fresh in her mind.

At full magnification, a few centers of population ap
peared, but they seemed hardly more than villages. A
Adolph Gondar had stated, they were concentrated along
the southwest shore of the long peninsula.

Adolph Gondar was summoned from his cabin; with
poor grace he indicated the exact location of his previous
landing. "I wouldn't land there again," he said in a surly
voice. "Try further south; the people are much more hospitable."

"I understood that they took little notice, of any sor
whatever."

"I've advised you; now you must do as you think best.'
Adolph Gondar stalked back to his cabin.

Bernard Bickel returned to the macro-viewer and made
a new study of the landscape.

"What do you think?" asked Dame Isabel.

"There doesn't seem to be as many villages farther
south. The countryside seems somewhat less fertile."

"We will land at the previous site," Dame Isabel decided. "I see no reason to be intimidated by Mr. Gondar's
ambiguous hints."

Afternoon moved across the face of Rlaru; sunset had
arrived before the *Phoebus* settled to a landing, almost
exactly at Adolph Gondar's original point of contact. En-
vironmental checks were made, and as before indicated
complete compatibility with the human metabolism.

During the checks Dame Isabel examined the countryside from the vantage of the bridge. Though she noted
several nearby villages, she saw none of the inhabitants,
and no one came to investigate the *Phoebus*. When she
alighted, with others of the company close behind, she
found only a small river meandered a few hundred yards
to the north; low hills rolled across the eastern horizon. In
certain quarters were trees, growing in rather irregular
rows, like a carelessly arranged orchard, while the
meadow to the south seemed to be planted with low
bushy shrubs. In general it was a pleasant peaceful landscape, with an air of long habitude.

With the deepening of darkness a sprinkle of lights

shone from the direction of the village, but these soon flickered and disappeared, and it seemed that only the company of the *Phoebus* was awake to enjoy the nocturnal quiet.

Dame Isabel ordered the setting of a routine watch and one by one the company retired inside the ship, some to bed, some to the saloon.

Dame Isabel and Bernard Bickel were almost the last to return within. Finally they did so, and Roger, standing a little apart, thought himself alone. But there was a stir nearby, and peering through the darkness he saw Madoc Roswyn. She came to stand beside him. "This is such a soothing place, Roger," she said. "So calm and quiet . . ." For a moment she looked off toward the dark village, then impulsively turned to Roger. "I've been extremely wicked, Roger. And you've been very kind to me. I'm ashamed. Truly I am."

"Don't let's talk about it," said Roger.

"But I must! It haunts me! Now that it's over I can see myself for the monomaniac I was."

"I'm sure you didn't mean to hurt anyone."

Madoc Roswyn laughed a soft forlorn laugh. "The sad truth is that I didn't care—which may be worse."

Roger could think of nothing to say which did not sound either prim or unnecessarily self-abnegatory. Madoc Roswyn seemed to interpret his silence as implacability and moved slowly away toward the entry-ramp. "Wait!" cried Roger, Madoc Roswyn obediently returned. "What I want to know," he said, stumbling over his words, "is what you're going to do now?"

"I don't know. I'll return to Earth, and I suppose find a job somewhere."

"The only lasting effect of this business," grumbled Roger, "is the state of my reflexes. I feel like a laboratory rat. When he presses a green button cheese comes down a chute; until suddenly pressing the green button gets him only shocks and air-jets."

Madoc Roswyn took his hand. "What if I asked you to push the green button just once more, and promised nothing but cheese and never any shocks and air-jets for the poor young rat again?"

"In that case," said Roger, "I'd push all the green buttons in my cage, every one I could find."

"Well—I promise."

Chapter Thirteen

DAWN CAME fresh and clear to Rlaru. The sun, somewhat larger and a deeper gold than Earth's sun, rose over the distant hills.

Not long after, some of the local inhabitants were seen: a half dozen men in blue trousers, white jackets and extremely wide-brimmed hats, on their way to work in a nearby field. Noticing the *Phoebus*, they paused in mild curiosity, then continued on the way, glancing back over their shoulders.

"Odd," muttered Dame Isabel. "Their lack of interest is almost insulting."

"Did you notice their physical characteristics?" asked Bernard Bickel. "Extremely man-like—yet in some subtle, almost indefinable, manner, not quite men."

"This is no surprise," said Dame Isabel, with a trace of asperity. "They are precisely the type of the Ninth Company. There can no longer be any doubt as to Mr. Gondar's complete veracity, at least in regard to the Ninth Company and Rlaru."

"None whatever," agreed Bernard Bickel. "As I recall, he spoke of three castes or classes: the indigents, the workers and the artists who constitute an elite."

"Yes, I recall a remark to this effect. Presumably a deputation will shortly come out to greet us."

But morning became noon and no one appeared but three or four men wearing coarse gray smocks and cloth sandals. Squatting in the dirt, they gave the *Phoebus* a brief inspection, then rising moved off in a purposeless amble, to disappear in a grove of trees beside the river.

151

Dame Isabel paced back and forth in front of the *Phoebus*, looking first toward the village, then shading her eyes with her hand and peering toward the workers in the field. Finally she returned into the ship and ascended to Adolph Gondar's cabin.

There was no response to her knock.

She knocked again, peremptorily. "Mr Gondar, open if you please."

Still no answer. After one further rap, Dame Isabel tried the door, but found it locked.

Nearby, on the bridge, sat the crew-man deputed to guard Adolph Gondar's cabin; Dame Isabel spoke sharply, "Fetch Mr. Henderson at once, and then ask Mr. Bickel to step up. I fear that Mr. Gondar may be ill."

The Chief Technician appeared. After a knock or two, he forced the door. Adolph Gondar was not in his cabin.

Dame Isabel turned ominously upon the crew-man who had been standing guard. "How and when did Mr. Gondar leave his cabin."

"I don't know. I'm sure I don't. He took his lunch; I saw it handed in to him, and that's only been an hour ago. I haven't had my eyes off that door. A cat couldn't have slipped out."

"Bernard," said Dame Isabel crisply, "please check the lifeboats."

Bernard Bickel shortly returned to report that all lifeboats were securely in their pods. Nor could Adolph Gondar have used the exit-ramp; those standing in front of the ship would have seen him. Dame Isabel ordered a search of the ship.

Adolph Gondar was not aboard. By some means unknown he had departed his cabin, seemingly vanishing into thin air.

In the middle afternoon the field workers in their odd broad-brimmed hats halted work and returned to the village. As before they gave the *Phoebus* a mildly interested inspection, though hardly slackening their pace to do so. Only Dame Isabel's sense of fitness prevented her from marching forth to demand a responsible delegation from the village. She watched the retreating backs a minute or two, then turned to Bernard Bickel and Andrei Szinc, who stood beside her. "What, in your expert opinions," she asked, "would seem an appropriate work to perform here, presuming we were able to attract an audience of other than bumpkins and vagabonds?"

Andrei Szinc flung out his hands, as if to imply that one opera would do as well as another for folk so incurious as these. Bernard Bickel replied to the same effect: "I find it difficult to decide. Frankly, I had expected a far different cultural complex—an ambiance considerably more lively and sophisticated."

"My feelings exactly," said Andrei Szinc. He looked around the landscape. Drenched in the golden haze of late afternoon it seemed wonderfully tranquil and beautiful, though permeated with a sense of remoteness and even melancholy, like a scene remembered from one's youth.

Frowning, Andrei Szinc spoke on slowly. "There seems an aimlessness here, a lack of purpose, as if people and landscape aren't altogether real. Perhaps 'archaic' is the word I want. Everything exudes a redolence of something old and half-forgotten."

Dame Isabel chuckled drily. "I admit Rlaru is not quite as I expected it—but both of you seem to have evaded my questions."

Bernard Bickel laughed and pulled at his fine gray mustache. "I evade because I am at a loss. I talk, hoping to stimulate an idea into existence—but I have failed. Still, for an off-the-cuff suggestion, why not *Tales of Hoffman*? Or perhaps *The Magic Flute* once more? Or even *Hansel and Gretel*?"

Andrei Szinc nodded. "Any of these would be suitable."

"Good," said Dame Isabel. "Tomorrow we will perform *Hansel and Gretel* in the open, and hope that the sound of the music, which we will amplify and direct toward the village, will attract an audience. Andrei, please see to bringing out the requisite sets, and arranging some sort of a curtain. Bernard, perhaps you would be good enough to inform Sir Henry and his people."

The company, which had become somewhat edgy, reacted with great energy to the prospect of a performance. Musicians and singers joined the crew in the labor of carrying out sets and stage properties, and rigging a makeshift curtain. Work continued by floodlight long after dark, and Dame Isabel noted with satisfaction that in the village lights were not extinguished as early as the night before, and occasionally lights which had been turned off came back to life.

There still was no clue as to what had become of Adolph Gondar. Various theories were current, most to the effect that Gondar, after leaving the ship by some crafty method, had made his way to the village in order to seek out his old acquaintances. It was generally expected that Gondar in his own good time would return to the ship.

* * * * * * *

On the next morning almost a dozen folk came out from the village, and now the *Phoebus* company for the first time saw the so-called "aristocrats" of Rlaru. These were people closely resembling in style and attitude the Ninth Company which Adolph Gondar had brought to Earth: slender well-shaped people of great grace, verve, and gaiety. They wore garments of various rich colors, no two of which were alike, and several carried musical instruments of the sort used by the Ninth Company.

Dame Isabel advanced to meet them, holding up her hands in the universal gesture of friendship—a gesture, however, which the folk of Rlaru did not seem to comprehend, for all appeared somewhat puzzled.

Dame Isabel, having established her peaceful intentions, spoke slowly and distinctly. "Hello, my friends of Rlaru. Are any of you members of the Ninth Company which visited Earth? Ninth Company? Earth?"

None of the natives gave any sign of understanding, though all listened with courtesy.

Dame Isabel tried once more. "We are musicians from Earth. We come to perform here on Rlaru as your wonderful Ninth Company performed on Earth. This afternoon we will bring you one of our great operas, *Hansel and Gretel,* by Englebert Humperdinck." She ended on a note of rather desperate cheerfulness. "We hope you will all come and bring your friends."

The villagers spoke a few grave words among themselves, turned to inspect the sets, and presently moved off about their affairs.

Dame Isabel looked after them with a dubious expression. "I hoped to convey an inkling, at least, of our purpose," she told Bernard Bickel. "I fear I did not succeed."

"Don't be too pessimistic," said Bernard Bickel. "Some of these alien races are wonderfully adept when it comes to sensing one's basic intents."

"Do you think then that we'll have an audience?"

"I wouldn't be surprised one way or the other."

Three hours after the sun reached the meridian Sir Henry took the orchestra into the first notes of the overture, and the stately horn chorale, amplified to a certain extent, sounded throughout the countryside.

The first of the Rlaru natives to appear were a group of smock-clad indigents, who came blinking out of the grove by the river as if the music had awakened them from sleep. About twenty of these wandered close and settled themselves into the last row of the benches. Then a dozen or so workmen from nearby fields came to investigate. Five or six stayed to watch and listen, while the others returned to their tasks. Dame Isabel sniffed in contempt. "Louts are louts, no matter where they are found."

During Scene Five a straggle of villagers appeared, including several aristocrats, to Dame Isabel's great satisfaction. During the whole of the second act there were perhaps forty persons in the audience, including the semi-torpid indigents, whom the workmen and aristocrats quite noticeably avoided.

"All considered," Dame Isabel told Sir Henry, Andrei

Szinc and Bernard Bickel after the performance, "I am well-pleased. The audience seemed to like what they saw."

"Not having Gondar puts us to great inconvenience," said Bernard Bickel fretfully. "I assume that he knows the language, and he would have been of great help in explaining our program."

"We will do without him," said Dame Isabel. "If any of the Ninth Company are here—as well they may be— surely they know at least a smattering of our language. We will demonstrate that Adolph Gondar is not as indispensable as he thinks he is."

"Certainly a mystery where the fellow got to," declared Sir Henry. "He never left by the off-ramp—that I'll swear to. I was standing at the bottom every minute, and I saw no sign of him."

"He'll no doubt return when he's good and ready," said Dame Isabel. "I refuse to worry about him. Tomorrow: *Les Contes d'Hoffmann,* and let us hope that today's performance will bring us a larger audience!"

* * * * * * *

Dame Isabel's hopes were abundantly fulfilled. As soon as the first notes of music drifted across the countryside, folk approached from all directions and settled on the benches without diffidence. The three castes Adolph Gondar had described could easily be distinguished by their costumes. The indigents, in their shapeless gray smocks sat to the side like pariahs. The workers wore blue or white pantaloons, blue, white or brown jackets and, more often then not, broad-brimmed headgear. The "aristocrats," of course, were as extravagant as peacocks among crows; only natural elegance and a certain playful hauteur lent credulity to their costumes. Several carried musical instruments, which they stroked or played softly, with apparently unconscious movements.

Dame Isabel watched in complete satisfaction. "This," she told Bernard Bickel, "is almost precisely what I had hoped for, Rlaru is by no means as technically advanced as I had presumed, but the folk here are sensitive and aware, in every stratum of society, which is more than can be said of Earth!"

Bernard Bickel had no dispute with her comments.

"After the performance," said Dame Isabel, "I will approach some of them, and inquire as to Mr. Gondar. It's quite possible that he has taken refuge with friends, and I would like to learn his intentions."

But when Dame Isabel tried to communicate with certain of the "aristocrats," she encountered only blank stares of incomprehension. "Mr. Gondar," spoke Dame Isabel, very distinctly. "I am interested in learning the whereabouts of Mr. Adolph Gondar. Do you know him?"

But the aristocrats moved courteously away. Dame Isabel clicked her tongue in exasperation. "Mr. Gondar could so easily have sent us word," she complained to Bernard Bickel. "Now we are left on tenterhooks . . . Well, evidently he knows his own business best." She looked across the meadow to where Roger and Madoc Roswyn were returning from a visit to the riverbank. "Now it seems that Roger has once more taken up with Miss Roswyn. I can't sat that I approve, but he has not troubled to ask my advice." She heaved a sigh. "But I am sure that the world will never go precisely to my liking."

"Does it for anyone?" asked Bernard Bickel with good-natured cynicism.

"Probably not, and I must reconcile myself to the fact. We had better discuss tomorrow's performance with Andrei. I must jack him up in regard to his costumes; today they were quite out of press."

Bernard Bickel accompanied her to the stage, and stood politely aside while Dame Isabel particularized on what she considered the deficiencies of the costuming.

As for Roger, the world was going almost precisely to his liking. Madoc Roswyn, now that her obsessions were spent, had become quieter, at once more reserved and more confiding, and in Roger's estimation, more appealing than ever. They had walked across the meadow to the river, to stroll along the bank. Poplar-like trees with mauve foliage rose above them; dendrons trailed black fronds into the water. A quarter-mile upstream a copse of tall dark trees surrounded what seemed a crumble of ruins. There was no sign of life, no movement, no sound, and presently, in a somewhat subdued mood, they turned away and returned through the golden afternoon to the *Phoebus*.

On the next day *The Magic Flute* was performed, to an even larger audience than the day before, and Dame Isabel was highly pleased. At the final curtain she stepped forth, addressed the audience at large, thanking them for their interest. Briefly she summarized the aims of the expedition, and, as the audience began to depart, inquired for news of Adolph Gondar. But if any among the audience understood her, they gave no acknowledgment.

The next afternoon, for *The Flying Dutchman*, attendance dwindled markedly. Dame Isabel was disturbed, both by the scantiness of the audience and their polite indifference to all her friendly overtures. "I hardly like to use the word 'ingratitude,'" she complained. "The fact remains that we have gone to great trouble and expense, without the slightest acknowledgment on their part. And today, a perfectly grand performance is played to a shadow of an audience, for the most part composed of the lower classes."

"Conceivably some special occasion has detained the aristocrats," Bernard Bickel suggested.

"But what of the working class? They are not bothering to attend the performances either. We are playing almost entirely to tramps and vagabonds!"

"I notice they listen at least as attentively as the workers, who seem almost bored," said Bernard Bickel.

"Perhaps they have nothing better to do," sniffed Dame Isabel.

"I've also seen the tramps or vagabonds, whatever they are, half-asleep," said Andrei Szinc. "I believe they're drug addicts, and carry their doses in those little pomander bags at their waists."

"That's an interesting thought," said Dame Isabel. "I've never seen them 'take a dip,' as the expression goes, but this of course means nothing. If true, both their lassitude and the ostracism they appear to suffer is explained." She reflected a moment. "I have noticed the little balls they carry, but I never considered the possibility of drugs . . . Hmmm . . . I wonder if we perhaps shouldn't bar them from our performances. We might recover some of our audience."

Bernard Bickel frowned dubiously. "I've never noticed any disesteem between the classes; indeed they ignore each other as completely as they do us."

"The whereabouts of Mr. Gondar poses another problem," said Dame Isabel peevishly. "If anyone knows what has happened to him, they clearly do not intend to inform us."

"Which implies one of two things," said Bernard Bickel. "Either he has met an unfortunate end, or Gondar himself does not wish information to reach us. In either case we are powerless."

"That certainly sums up the situation," said Dame Isabel slowly. "I confess that I am considering an early return to Earth. We have more than fulfilled our ambitions, especially here on Rlaru—although it would be rewarding to receive some sort of acknowledgment."

"Yes, the folk here certainly are—well, languid, when it comes to expressing appreciation," Bernard Bickel agreed.

"Tomorrow we will do *Parsifal*," said Dame Isabel. "Sir Henry suggested *The Marriage of Figaro*, but I fear it would be too slight, directly following *Fliegende Holländer*."

"On the other hand, there's always the risk of tedium," said Bernard Bickel, "especially for persons not imbued with the Wagnerian mystique."

"I consider it a calculated risk," stated Dame Isabel. "The level of musical sophistication is high, we must not forget this."

"Which makes today's fall-off in attendence all the
more peculiar," said Bernard Bickel.

* * * * * * *

The following day brought thunderheads drifting in
from the west, and it seemed as if a storm were in the offing. But the wind shifted, the clouds veered to the south,
and the sun shone down from a magically fresh sky.

In spite of Dame Isabel's hopes, the audience for *Parsifal* was pitiably small, consisting of three or four aristocrats and a score of the indigents. This expression of
apathy infuriated Dame Isabel, and she gave serious
thought to ending the performance at the end of the first
act. She also considered sending Roger over to the village
to urge more of the local inhabitants to attend the performance. Theatrical tradition forbade the first course;
her inability to find Roger prevented the second.

To her further annoyance the already sparse audience
began to dwindle. One by one, as if answering some
unheard summons they rose from their seats and sidled
off around the ship. Finally the three aristocrats departed,
leaving only half a dozen pariahs. This was too much for
Dame Isabel. She sent Bernard Bickel after the aristocrats, to try to persuade them to sit the performance out,
if only from the courtesy to the singers. Without enthusiasm Bickel went off on his mission, to return five minutes
later, grim and angry. "Come with me a moment," he told
Dame Isabel. "I want you to see for yourself."

Dame Isabel followed him to the far side of the *Phoebus*, and there, in the halcyon light of the afternoon sun,
sat the Tough Luck Jug Bank, playing in all its raucous
fervor. In an attentive circle sat thirty or forty of the pariahs and somewhat to the rear as many aristocrats. Nearby
stood Roger and Madoc Roswyn and most of the crew.

In speechless indignation Dame Isabel listened while
The Tough Luck Jug Band rendered a tune which seemed
to be called *You Gotta See Mama Every Night*. There
were several verses, as many more instrumental choruses,
each more unrestrained than the last.

Dame Isabel glanced at Bernard Bickel; he shook his head in disgust. Together they turned back to the sorry spectacle. Four or five more of the pariahs came from around the *Phoebus*; the opera apparently was being played to empty seats. Dame Isabel shouted into Bernard Bickel's ear: "If this represents the level of local taste, we might as well return to Earth at once!"

Bernard Bickel gave a curt nod; once again they listened as *You Gotta See Mama* reached a crescendo. The whole band joined to sing a final chorus; Dame Isabel leaned slightly backward. Total vulgarity, total clatter! Rhythmic, even amusing, she thought, if one had inclinations in this direction. Admittedly the music—if such it could be called—did somehow manage to counteract and even vanquish the pervasive melancholy of the world . . . Dame Isabel noticed that each of the indigents held his little leather sphere, or pomander ball, carefully in his lap. After such a performance, she told herself bitterly, they would need all their drugs and narcotics indeed!

The music rambled through a clattering rattling coda and slammed to a halt. The Tough Luck Jug Band sat back, apparently pleased with themselves. The aristocrats muttered together in something like awe. The indigents sighed, and once again their gazes became unfocused.

Dame Isabel marched forward. "What is the meaning of this?" she cried in a ringing voice.

The Tough Luck Jug Band did not bother to reply. Hastily gathering their instruments they departed around the ship. Dame Isabel forced her unwilling features into an expression of affability, and turned to the audience. "You must come back to the opera! We are performing for your benefit, and we expect you to enjoy it. These buffoons will not be back, I assure you." With Bernard Bickel's help she herded as many of the group as possible back to the outdoor theater.

Resigning themselves the natives huddled on the benches, and so the final act passed. Directly upon the fall of the curtain stewards came fortified with trays of *petits-fours* and pitchers of lemonade. Dame Isabel motioned the aristocrats to help themselves: "They're ever so good, I'm sure you'll enjoy them!"

But the aristocrats politely departed.

Dame Isabel wheedled and coaxed, but not even the pariahs would approach the refreshments. At last she flung up her hands in defeat. "Very well, you must do as you like, although I simply can't understand why you don't appreciate what we're doing for you."

The oldest of the indigents absently fingered the little palps or flaps of his leather sphere. He looked among his fellows, as if engaging in unspoken communication, then turned his eyes upon Dame Isabel. She felt a curious electric thrill. "Watch," he seemed to be telling her. "Watch and then go your way." He squeezed the little leather ball. Bernard Bickel gasped; Dame Isabel swung about, and found the sky to be dancing with colored shapes. They mingled and separated, merged inward and outward and settled to the meadow which became a place of luminous magic, and the whole *Phoebus* company came front in awe to watch the magnificences now displayed to them. Cities like flower gardens appeared one after the other, as if in compendium: each different, each a development of the last, each with its own delights and prideful vistas, each receding and growing remote. A miscellany of new images appeared in the foreground: regattas of boats with enormous patterned sails, each of which might have been alive and sentient: a jeweled moth. Exalted figures marched in a stately pavanne; there were tourneys of love and beauty, gusts and whispers of many musics. Now came a series of pageants, performances by troupes like the Ninth Company, and Dame Isabel thought to recognize the Ninth Company itself. Suddenly there was silence, so intense as to be an ecstatic sensation in itself. Down from the sky floated a battered space-ship: it landed and Adolph Gondar, or rather a caricature of Adolph Gondar alighted. The Ninth Company sauntered by in their sumptuous garments; Adolph Gondar seemed to pounce like a spider; with the aid of faceless helpers he roughly herded the Ninth Company aboard his ship, which at once departed, and once again there was silence. The episode fleeted past with exceeding swiftness; Adolph Gondar seemed more comic than evil: a travesty of wickedness, and the whole episode was no more than a wry footnote, a mordant little jest which the *Phoebus* company could enjoy or not as they felt inclined.

There followed other spectacles and vistas, and these seemed far away and long past, like memories half-forgotten. A parade of dead heroes came by, turning to search the faces of those who watched, as if asking for knowledge which had been denied them. All seemed to ask the same question, and then they were gone from view. Cities were built and listlessly abandonded: all goals had been achieved, all excellences attained. Nothing remained but idleness, casual amusement . . . Finally in gigantic enlargement appeared The Tough Luck Jug Band, with its music of boldness and assertion, enthusiasm conquering surfeit. For a brief space the world was renewed and wonderful things seemed possible. Then the meadow was as before, the sky was blank; the *Phoebus* company stood alone beside the ship.

Everyone returned within. Dame Isabel went to the saloon and ordered a pot of strong tea. Bernard Bickel and Sir Henry joined her, but no one was inclined to make conversation. Dame Isabel felt confused and resentful. In a sense she had been mocked and ridiculed, though in a dispassionate and even kindly fashion . . . Why had not the folk of Rlaru explained themselves before she had presented her program? Clearly they had no need of anything the *Phoebus* could offer—except the Tough Luck Jug Band. Obviously folk of rather vulgar inclinations, thought Dame Isabel sourly. Their old fineness of discrimination had apparently died . . . And yet—no, of course not. Impossible. Dame Isabel resolutely ordered her thinking. A person must establish a definite set of verities, she told herself, and definitely abide by them, no matter how questionable these same verities. She drank her tea, set the cup into the saucer with a resolute click. Bernard Bickel and Sir Henry drew themselves up in their chairs, as if heartened by the sound. "We have no further business here on Rlaru," said Dame Isabel. "We will leave in the morning." Summoning Andrei Szinc she gave orders for all stage properties to be stowed inside the ship.

"What of Adolph Gondar?" asked Bernard Bickel.

"It is clear that he committed a wrong against these people," said Dame Isabel. "Clearly he had been warned never again to approach Rlaru; when he did so he was punished. His fate is out of our hands."

"Could they spirit him out of his cabin?" demanded Bernard Bickel incredulously. "Through the solid walls of the ship?"

"Why not?" Dame Isabel demanded sharply. "It is amply clear that they brought the Ninth Company back from Earth; why should they not extract Mr. Gondar from his cabin?"

"It is beyond my understanding," said Bernard Bickel.

"And mine as well."

* * * * * * *

Roger looked through the ship: saloon, bridge, every place he could think of, but Madoc Roswyn was nowhere to be found. He went down the ramp, looked back and forth, then circled the ship. Madoc Roswyn sat by herself watching the sunset. Roger, still not certain that he understood her moods, started to beat an inconspicuous retreat, but she called to him, and so he joined her. Without words they watched dusk settle over the countryside. Two gaunt silhouettes passed across the afterglow: from their garments and gait a pair of the vague-eyed men Adolph Gondar had described as "vagabonds."

Madoc Roswyn spoke in a low voice, so that Roger had to bend to hear her. "They could destroy all their knowledge, forget all their power; they could move to a new planet; they could begin all over. I wonder why they don't."

Roger could provide no information, and they watched the two figures wander off into the dusk. A cool breeze began to blow in from the sea; they rose to their feet and started back around the ship. And now another dark shape appeared against the sky: a tall half-running, half-stumbling figure emitting hoarse panting cries. "It's Gondar!" said Roger. "He's alive!"

Adolph Gondar rushed past them, pressed his hands against the ship and gave a great sob of relief. Unsteadily he made his way to the entrance-port with Roger and Madoc Roswyn coming behind. At the port, with what seemed to be his final reserves of strength, he drew himself upright, threw back his shoulders and summoning all his dignity, staggered up the ramp.

* * * * * * *

In the saloon, after he had eaten ravenously, Adolph Gondar told his story. As Dame Isabel had speculated, he had been warned never again to visit Rlaru. He had hoped that by keeping to his cabin he would remain unnoticed, but such was not the case. He had been snatched out into the night, tossed back and forth through clouds, wind, sleet and rain, dropped into the ocean, lifted, flung twenty miles head over heels, and finally dropped into a thicket of coarse furze. For days he had wandered and finally from the ridge of a distant hill had spied the *Phoebus.*

Dame Isabel was not inclined to be sympathetic. "You are lucky to escape so easily!" she told him sternly. "Your conduct was no less than piratical; you kidnaped twenty persons without the slightest intent of returning them to their homes."

"Not at all!" Adolph Gondar protested, "I planned to send them back after we had earned enough money. I told them so, which is the only reason they agreed to perform."

"There naturally will be no question as to the disposition of the money," said Dame Isabel. "Under no circumstances will you be allowed to profit by what, at the most lenient interpretation, was an unethical act. The money involved is barely enough to cover costs of the present tour, and I can think of no better use for it."

Adolph Gondar threw up his hands in despair and tottered off to his cabin.

The following morning as the sun rose above the low hills, the *Phoebus* departed Rlaru. Logan de Appling fed the coordinates of Earth into the computer; Rlaru fell behind. The golden sun dimmed, became one among the stars and presently was lost.

Chapter Fourteen

THE DAY after the return of the *Phoebus* to Earth, Dame Isabel held a press conference on the terrace of her beautiful home Ballew. "The tour, in general, was a resounding success," she told the assembled journalists. "Beyond question it contributed to the culture and understanding of all those before whom we performed."

Bernard Bickel, who was also present, concurred with the statement. "As might be expected there were various levels of comprehension, corresponding to what I call the 'cultural perspective' of the peoples who formed our various audiences. They learned much from us, and we from them. I am sure we have enhanced the musical reputation of Earth."

"What of Rlaru?" called someone. "Does it exist? Or was Adolph Gondar a fraud?"

"There was never any uncertainty in this regard," Dame Isabel replied coldly. "I informed you that the world existed; this assurance should have been enough."

"Then you visited Rlaru?"

"Yes indeed; this was one of the goals of our tour. The world is not as stimulating as might have been expected. We gave several performances which were well received, though the inhabitants do not display a notoriously high level of taste."

"Tell us more about Rlaru. Are there theaters? Music-halls?"

"Nothing like that. At the moment I do not care to discuss the matter further. My nephew Roger Wool is writ-

167

ing a book describing the voyage in detail, and if you need further information, you will find it here."

Roger Wool was indeed very busy, with his new wife, Mrs. Madoc Wool, providing invaluable assistance. The world was in a very satisfactory state, reflected Roger. His aunt's wealth had been restored to its previous state, and he stood to make a substantial sum from the publication of his book. It was always possible, of course, that Dame Isabel might embark on some new and even more expensive project, but this was one of the hazards of living. Occasionally watching his bride an even darker apprehension came to trouble him: what if she should meet a man of her own race? She had assured him that none remained on Earth, but what of Yan? And Roger's thoughts would fly far, far across space to a stretch of stony barren beside a dark forest where stood a ruined piano . . . Small chance, Roger told himself, small chance.